Praise for Emily Harper

"Emily Harper does an amazing job of making the reader connect with the characters and in turn you feel every spark... Can't wait to see what she has in store for us next."- Amazon Review

Praise for White Lies

"If you're in the mood for something light that will tickle your funny-bone, join the bumbling, romantic Natalie as she searches for her perfect man. She's endearingly hilarious. I loved it."- Magnolia Blossoms Review

"The story bounces along, sweeping the reader up along with it, and has a feel-good factor that makes it both unputdownable and downright fantastic. Natalie is incredibly likeable, with Harper nailing the common female trait of overthinking things, making her relatable in a very normal sort of way. Oliver, er love interest, is knee wobblingly perfect: handsome, driven and conflicted – what more could you want in a book boyfriend!"- Best Chick Lit

"White Lies was a very fun read, easily devoured in one sitting. You could see the growth Natalie goes through as she learns to be more honest and confident in her ideas and talents. She still remains cute, bubbly, and fun, like that best friend who knows all the good gossip."- Readers' Favorite

Checking Inn

EMILY HARPER

ISBN: 099209531X
ISBN-13: 978-0992095314

To my partner in crime, Jennifer Sully.
It's hard for me to remember a time that we weren't best
friends, and I wouldn't have it any other way.

ACKNOWLEDGMENTS

Thank you to my family and friends, your support means more to me than words can express. To my editor, Emily Ferko, you know I would be hopeless without you. And finally, to David, Ava and Noah, it's all for you.

One

"You know Kate, this whole thing would be a lot easier if you would stop fidgeting."

"I'm not fidgeting, I just want to make sure you're doing it right," I say.

"It will be perfect, don't worry."

That's the problem– I always worry. I worry about Mr. Shaw in suite 204 who keeps sneaking a dog into his room. I worry about the guest in room 210 that says she might have seen a ghost last night; that, or Mrs. Phelps was wandering the hall in her dressing gown. I worry that the caterers are going to run out of food or drop it all on the floor and we won't have anything to serve. I worry that the housekeeper, Luisa, actually knows more English than she lets on, and has just been toying with me for years. I worry. It's who I am.

"I just want everything to go smoothly this weekend. If Samantha Manning writes a bad review..." I tell myself not to hyperventilate; I don't have time for a panic attack. "She didn't look impressed when she checked in yesterday."

"She won't write a bad review because

everything is perfect. You made sure it is."

Of course everything is perfect. I don't do anything that *isn't* perfect. It's not that I am *obsessive...* I just like everything to be at its best, and it just so happens that I am the only one that can make sure that it is. But I am *not* obsessive.

"The Inn looks fantastic; we are fully booked for the whole weekend, and the dinner was amazing last night. Everything will be fine," Tracy assures me.

"Right, you're right," I say. "This is the last thing on my list."

I live my life by lists. I make a list every night of all the things I need to do the next day and put it on a clipboard. And I know it has become a running joke around here, but I love my clipboard. Every year at Christmas I go out and treat myself to a new one. When I rip off the cellophane and smell the mixture of plywood and metal, I literally have to control myself. Last year I bought a new pen on the same day– it was too much.

"Okay, just hold your thigh back like this," Tracy says, taking my hand and showing me what to do.

"Like this?" I ask to make sure.

She nods her head and turns to pick something up off the table.

"On a scale of one to ten, this is what– like a four?" I ask.

"It depends. If you get someone who is good at it, it shouldn't hurt too much."

"You're good at it, right?" This is the real reason why I'm here. It's not that I don't trust Tracy. She said she was good, and I believe her.

But, I trust myself more.

"The best," she says. "But, if you keep moving, it's not going to be even."

"Sorry, " I say, and readjust my hand exactly as she showed me.

"Okay, it's just like ripping off a Band Aid," she says, and I try not to look panicked at the word 'ripping'. "Just relax and stay very still."

"Right," I nod.

"On three. One, two," the sound of my phone causes a knee jerking reaction as I attempt to sit up.

"Sorry, sorry!" I say when Tracy pushes back my leg to look at what damage my movement caused. "I just need to get that, could you—"

"Kate, time is of the essence when you are doing this. It will take five minutes. I'm sure it can wait five minutes."

"Maybe," I look at my phone doubtfully. "But, that's the front desk."

"Give me five minutes," Tracy says, and her stern look makes me give in.

"Okay, you're right. Sorry, keep going."

Tracy takes a deep breath and moves my thigh back.

"Okay, on three. One, two–"

The shrill ring from my pager rolls around the room, making both of us jump, and Tracy's hand pulls back– the ripping sound fills the room.

"Oh my God!" I scream while Tracy tries to apply pressure to my scarlet colored skin.

"I told you it was going to hurt if you moved," she argues.

"Why would women ever do that to themselves?" I groan, trying to lift my head to look at the injured area.

"It gets better; the first pull is always the most painful."

"Really?" I ask skeptically.

"Absolutely, it's basic psychology. Freud, I think," Tracy says while adding more wax to the stick. "Now you will be expecting the worst and it won't be so bad."

"Are you sure? I think Freud was the one who came up with *repressing* memories."

"Maybe it was another one, but the point is it's scientific," she says.

"Alright fine, we'll keep going. Right after I call the front desk–"

"No. We are finishing this now or we're never

going to get it done." Tracy shakes her head while blowing on the hot wax. "It's not like it's a life or death problem; someone probably doesn't know where the extra napkins are. Why don't you try and think of something else to get your mind off of it? It might help you relax a little."

Tracy obviously doesn't know me very well. I'm humanly incapable of relaxing. And how is anyone supposed to relax while their skin is being forcefully removed from their body?

I really don't have time for this today. I really don't. But with Samantha's review hanging over my head, it's something that needs to be done. I know she goes to the spa all the time, and of course it's only logical that she would try ours while she's here.

I like to be thorough with the Inn: personally inspecting every room before a new guest arrives, observing the rush at dinner time, and with the new spa expansion I thought it was a good idea to try out the services to make sure there weren't any kinks to iron out. Though why I thought I needed to try *waxing* is beyond me...

No, I know why everything has to be perfect. Two words: Samantha Manning.

Because, if last night was any indication, she's looking for a reason to ruin my life.

And I can honestly say, I have absolutely no idea

why. We went to the same high school: she was the popular one, I was the dork. She got all the boys, and I got new clipboards. She moved to New York to become famous, and I stayed at home to keep an eye on my free-spirited mother. She became a famous hotel and restaurant critic, and I bought a small portion of an abandoned historical home and painstakingly restored it into a beautiful Inn that is now on the verge of bankruptcy. Well, at least it will be if this weekend doesn't go well.

The Inn's investors are going to want to see an immediate return on their investment, and in a town whose population would probably fit into one of those fancy condo buildings in Manhattan, instant results are hard to come by. Even so, Summerside is quickly becoming a quaint tourist attraction, especially in the warmer months. Located just outside of New York on the coast, it has good weather and great scenic views, without the high prices of the Hamptons and other vacation hot spots close to the city. But, the renovations of the old plantation-style mansion were more extensive than we had originally anticipated. We missed the summer crowd and as Autumn's breeze is fast encroaching, I had to rack my brains to come up with a solution.

So, I called Samantha. Well actually, I got my mother to talk to her mother, and she called

Samantha.

I'm still unsure if it was the right move, which is probably what is making me so crazy right now. I'm never *not* sure of anything. Or maybe it's the nasty looks that Samantha gave me last night, or the way she "accidently" spilled her drink all down the front of my dress.

It's a toss up.

I have to win her over though; one positive review from Samantha Manning will make this the most popular Inn for miles around. But, if she hates it here...

Well, let's say I hope my organs are in good shape because I might have to sell a few.

"That's good, I can see you're relaxing," Tracy says while smearing the wax on my skin.

I nearly laugh out loud. I'm sure I am the picture of relaxation.

"I'll relax when this weekend is over and we have our five star rating." I would even take a four at this point.

No, that's a lie. A four star rating would eat away at me for the rest of my life. I don't do anything by almost.

"I feel like I haven't seen Tim and the boys in days," Tracy says, putting the stick inside the waste bin. "That must be why *I'm* so relaxed lately."

"Oh please," I say. "You and Tim are more in love now than when you guys were crowned prom king and queen."

"It's a different kind of love now," Tracy reaches for the next strip of cotton. "Back then, you were in love with everything the person was going to be. After a while, you're in love with the person in spite of what they're not."

"Everyone was different in high school. I would be worried if nothing had changed."

"Things have changed alright," she says, looking down at her body. "Well, for some of us. You have the same great genes as your mother. Those killer cheekbones and green eyes. It also helps that you haven't had two kids."

I look down at my body; it's always been all legs. I have a great figure if I wanted to be a ballerina, which sounds great in theory, but I have no coordination and hardly any cleavage. Also, it's hard to get people to take you seriously when a small wind could knock you over.

"Some things change for the better though. I was such a bitch to you in high school— which I'm now mortified about," Tracy laughs, "and now I'm giving you your first bikini wax."

"Then why do I get the impression that you still hate me?" I look at the strip of cotton in Tracy's hand.

"You should be grateful; Tim says I have the hands of an angel." She leans forwards, her attention focused on placing the cotton strip in the right spot, but stops and looks apprehensively at me. "You know, I could talk to her if you want. I haven't seen Samantha in years, well except for last night, but she's a real piece of work. I mean, she was nasty in high school, but she seems to have developed an extra set of horns as she got older. If I mentioned we needed a good review…"

"No, I want the Inn to get a five-star rating because that is what it deserves. No favoritism," I say.

I don't count the chocolates I placed on her pillow last night as biasing the results. Or the gift basket full of handmade soap. Those were more 'welcome home' presents than please-don't-destroy-me bribes.

At least, that's what the rational part of my brain told the ethical part.

"Samantha should be down for breakfast any minute," I say. I can just imagine her walking down the oak staircase in deathly high heels, a tight mini dress, her long blond hair glistening. She's one of those women who never age, and when I saw her for the first time again yesterday I felt so… plain.

My hair has been overdue for highlights for the last two weeks, but with the Inn opening and the review, the task didn't make it onto my list.

My naturally curly hair is always secured in a bun on the back of my head anyways, so it doesn't actually look that bad. But when you are standing beside a goddess, roots don't help the situation.

I wear a black skirt suit to work from Monday to Thursday. Friday I wear a grey one (you know, get a bit crazy for the weekend). On Saturday and Sunday my mother insists that the staff be allowed to dress more casually, so she forces me into a pair of dress pants and a blouse.

Considering Mom wears kimonos everywhere she goes, someone has to be able to represent the Inn properly. My mother co-owns the Inn with me and the other investors, and helps me run the day to day operation. Though, most of the time I have to look after the Inn and fix whatever mess she's made of her daily tasks all on my own.

Which reminds me, I have to get to the front desk before my mother has a chance to introduce herself to Samantha. She was never fond of Samantha growing up, which either stems from her hatred for Samantha's mother or the fact Samantha made my life a living hell in school.

It really is a fifty-fifty call.

It took all my persuasive powers to convince Mom to speak to Mrs. Manning about securing a review.

My phone rings again and I stare at it while tapping my hand on the table.

Tracy looks at the clock and then rubs more vigorously on the cotton strip. "Okay, on three. One, two—"

The knock on the spa door causes both of us to turn, Tracy pulling off the next wax strip.

"Sweet Jesus!"

"Sorry, sorry," Tracy rushes to the door, opening it only a crack to look out. "Yes?"

"I need Miss Kate. *Now.*" I can hear Luisa's thick Spanish accent on the other side of the door.

"We're nearly done," Tracy says. "What's wrong?"

"I need her *muy rápido*," I can hear the panic in Luisa's voice and I start to sit up.

"What is it?" I say, getting up and putting one leg in my pants.

"Kate, you can't go when you're only half done. It looks horrible!" Tracy argues.

"No one's going to see it," I say.

"Well, if someone does, make sure you say you got it somewhere else. Or it's a new trend," she adds while I scramble to the door.

"Luisa, what is it?" I ask as I come around the door to look at the housekeeper.

Her face is drained of all color and I can see tears in her eyes.

"Luisa?"

"She is…" she starts, then swallows while grasping her handkerchief. "She was like that when I get there."

"What? Who?" I ask. When she doesn't reply I grab her arm. "What's going on?"

"That senorita, the review lady," Luisa says.

"Samantha Manning?" I ask.

Luisa nods.

"Well, what?" I ask, starting to get worried. Oh God, I hope Luisa didn't walk in on her naked or anything. The last thing I need right now is a sexual harassment claim.

"She's… *dead.*"

"What do you mean she's *dead?*" Tracy asks.

"She's dead!" Luisa yells hysterically. "Muerto! She goes to cielo! SHE'S DEAD!"

"She can't be dead; she hasn't written the review!" I yell.

Okay, that came out wrong.

"What I mean is, are you sure she's *dead?*" I ask.

Maybe dead means something different in Spanish. Like… really, *really* sick.

"Sí, I'm sure." Luisa says. "I go to her room to clean and knock on the door. She never answer, so I went in, and she is on the cama... dead."

"Maybe she was just... sleeping," Tracy suggests, and I nod in encouragement.

Luisa shakes her head and darts her eyes back to me. "I touched her," she cries and looks at her hands as though they are a foreign object. "I don't know what to do, should I try to breathe life back?"

I look to Tracy, but she looks as horrified as me.

"Her eyes stare at me with death," Luisa says with a faraway voice, looking at the wall between Tracy and myself.

"Oh God," I cry and put my shaking hand to my chest.

"What do I do?" Luisa asks.

"Well, we have to call the police," Tracy says.

"No, we can't call the police!" I say, looking frantically at both of them. "They will shut us down."

"Kate, I know this is a lot to process right now—" Tracy places her hand on my arm.

"You know, I know someone," Luisa says in a whispered tone.

"What do you mean?" Tracy asks.

"If Miss Kate needs the cuerpo to disappear," she says.

"You can't be serious!" Tracy yells.

Tracy looks at my eyes and throws her arms up when I don't immediately rebuke the suggestion. "Kate!"

"Okay, okay," I say, holding my hands up. "We will call the police. But we need to try and do this as discreetly as possible."

Luisa nods, turns around, and shuffles her feet back to the reception area.

Oh God, I can feel my chest tightening. My breath is coming in short gasps and I want to put my head between my knees. I look at Tracy with pleading eyes. "Tell me this won't ruin us."

"Of course not," Tracy says, putting a reassuring hand on my back. "We work in the hospitality industry, I'm sure this sort of thing happens more often than you would think."

Luisa reappears with the cordless phone and hands it to me.

"Okay," I say, nodding. I punch in the numbers 9-1-1 and put the phone to my ear.

"9-1-1, what's your emergency? Do you need fire, ambulance, or police?"

"Umm, all I think," I say. "Well, not fire. And not ambulance, because it's too late for that. So just police I guess," I say, my hysteria causing me to not think coherently. Really, I should have made a list to follow during emergency deaths. This is so unlike me.

"What's your emergency?"

"I run the Summerside Inn–"

"Kate?" the operator asks.

"Yes?"

"It's me, Suzanne!"

"Oh, hi Suzanne," I say. Suzanne is my mother's neighbor.

"How are you?" she asks, losing her professional telephone voice.

"Er, not great actually–"

"You know, I have been telling your mother for ages to get you to give me a call to see how Becky's working out there, and I bet she never even told you–"

"Listen, Suzanne. We have a bit of an emergency here…"

"Oh yes, of course," Suzanne has the professional voice again. "You need the police? What's wrong– vandalism? I just saw that nasty Sawyer boy hanging around the back of the supermarket smoking, and I bet you he–"

"No, it's nothing like that," I say. "It's one of our guests. They've umm… died."

I hear the gasp of shock on the other end of the phone, and my panic at what everyone else's reaction is going to be causes me to grasp the phone tighter.

"No! Oh, you poor thing." I can hear Suzanne type something into the computer. "What do you think was the cause of death?"

"What do you mean?" I ask.

"The cause of death. I need to know what you think might have happened to tell the police."

"Oh, right. Okay," I say and put my hand over the mouthpiece. "She wants to know what the cause of death is."

"How the hell should we know?" Tracy asks.

I shrug my shoulders and take my hand off the mouthpiece to talk to Suzanne when I hear Luisa say, "estrangulación."

"*What?*" Tracy and I yell together as I quickly try to cover the phone so Suzanne doesn't hear.

Oh please God, let that translate to "died peacefully in her sleep".

"Her neck is all bruised. I see the fingers marks on her throat," Luisa says in an ominous voice as she puts her own hands to her neck to demonstrate.

"Why the hell didn't you offer that little tidbit earlier?" Tracy yells, and I wave my hands to tell her to lower her voice.

"You never ask me!" Luisa says.

"Did she say *strangulation?*" I hear Suzanne's voice in my ear, and I honestly think I might pass out.

"We– she– we don't know," I say and look at Tracy's bewildered face. "Luisa may have seen something, but she's not sure."

"This is serious," Suzanne says, and continues typing. "I'm going to have to send out a team. Probably some detectives from Hartford. I'm not sure Summerside's police are able to deal with homicides."

"What is she saying?" Tracy asks as all the color drains from my face.

"They have to send out a team," I reply and shake my head.

"Don't let anyone leave the Inn. The police will want to talk with anyone who may have had contact with the victim."

The victim. Oh my God, we're finished.

"Kate?" Suzanne says when I don't respond.

"Of course, no one will leave." I reply.

And no one will ever come back, either.

Two

Okay, get it together Kate. You're a professional.

At least, this is what I keep telling myself as Tracy, Luisa, and I are huddled around the reception desk waiting for the police to arrive. I haven't told the other staff yet. I just told them we were having a fire and safety drill, and a bunch of emergency personnel are coming so we need to keep the hallways clear and encourage the guests to stay put for an hour or so. So far I think everyone has bought it.

We don't know for sure that Samantha was murdered. Luisa's English isn't very good, and she has been known to exaggerate from time to time. Maybe Samantha was just wearing a weird looking scarf...

I just don't want to alarm anyone. I mean, they could send one or two detectives out and that's it. No need to get everyone panicked about that.

Though, if SWAT shows up, I honestly think I will pass out.

The first thing I do when I get back behind the reception desk is have a good long inhale on my puffer. Then I start organizing. I put the pens back into their proper compartments based on color coding. I straighten the calculator and reservation book so they are exactly parallel to the desk's edge. I go over to the table where I keep the guest sign in book with little candies, and make sure everything is perfect there too. With every straight line and tidy surface I can feel my breathing return to normal.

I need to stay positive. I can't freak out. I have to be the leader here.

Right, positive thoughts... positive thoughts... like... umm... oh– maybe a nicer colleague of Samantha's will come to collect her things, see our fabulous Inn, and write a five-star review.

No, on second thought, it might be a little too soon to have positive thoughts.

It's better just to clear my mind.

Tracy squeezes my hand and I offer her a small smile of thanks.

Suzanne said the police would be here in a few minutes, and I keep darting my eyes around the parking lot. My eyes widen when I notice a blue sedan pull in and I run my hand through my hair.

"Oh, shit," I say and grab for my inhaler again.

"Are they here?" Tracy asks.

"Worse. It's my mother."

My mother is honestly the last thing I need right

now. I would take a bulldozer coming through the front door over my mother at this exact moment. For one, my mother is capable of more damage, and at least the insurance would cover the bulldozer. I know this because the insurance salesman talked my mom into getting every single possible thing covered when our insurance was up for renewal last year. He came in one day, when I was off sick (which I have made sure I have never been since then for this exact reason), talked her into the premium plan, and got her to sign on the spot. Now I have a three year term that costs a fortune to cancel, and my insurance rates are triple what they used to be. Though, if there is a tsunami which causes the Inn to flood, and a shark bites one of our guests, I can rest assured that we will be covered. The sad thing is, I am not even joking.

"She's coming in," Tracy says.

"No one can tell her what is going on." I peer through the glass to see how far away she is and turn back to the other two. "Swear to me you won't tell her."

"Kate, she's an owner of the Inn. She's going to find out," Tracy says.

"I know that," I say. "But I will tell her after the police have been here. If she finds out she will insist on being a part of the investigation; you know how she lives for the drama."

"There is a woman upstairs that has probably been murdered. Do you honestly think your mother can make the situation any worse than it already is?" Tracy frantically whispers so the guests in the library next to us won't hear.

I look at my mother who walks away from her car only to be jerked back as part of her flowing kimono is trapped in her car's door.

"Yes. Yes, I do. Not a word."

I turn as the door opens and see my mother's arms open wide. My mother has always had a great figure with lots of curves. The streak of grey at the front of her curly mop of hair gives her an artsy look that I know she loves.

"Kate, darling," she says. "Sorry I'm a bit late, I couldn't find my zen this morning."

"Not a problem," I say, and shove my inhaler in the drawer. I've had chronic asthma since I was six, but I try and only use the puffer in real emergencies. If she sees it, she will know something is wrong. "Actually, it's really slow today, so you can have the whole day off. Find all the zen you need."

My mother laughs and puts her bag down on top of the reservation book, scattering my neatly lined notepad and pencils in all directions.

"No need, I already found it." She smiles and lifts her eyebrows. "Did I walk in on a gossip fest?

There's nothing I love more than women huddled together with hushed tones, as nature intended us."

"We weren't talking about anything," I say, darting my eyes to the other girls. "We were just going over some things."

"Kate, I can always tell when you're lying because your nostrils flare," my mother says and turns to Tracy. "Were you talking about men? Kate never talks about men with me. Even Greg the Great. I still can't figure out why."

"Maybe it's because I've asked you a million times not to call him that," I say in an irritated tone.

"You still date that man?" Luisa says, and I shoot her an exasperated look for encouraging the conversation.

"They are days away from an engagement, aren't you darling?" My mother asks, and I have to clamp down my teeth to stop my response. Greg apparently hinted to my mother months ago that he was going to ask me to marry him, but he still hasn't proposed. I think my mother secretly enjoys every day that passes by. It's not that she doesn't like Greg. I mean, what's not to like? He's great.

"Tara! You said you weren't going to tell Kate he brought it up," Tracy says.

"I didn't tell her," my mother says. "She just looked at me and knew. I could never keep anything from her. It's kind of creepy actually."

It's true. Maybe it's because I learned at an early age that my mother has a tendency to get herself into *situations*. I also learned that I am the one that is going to have to fix it for her. I can just look at my mother and know she is hiding something. Then I make a list and use my deductive reasoning, and I can usually figure out what it is in under an hour. The marriage proposal took me seven minutes. It's my all-time best.

"Anyways, as I was saying before, we are really slow today..." I look to the others for encouragement.

"Isn't that girl here to write the review?" My mother asks, and I can feel all three of us go tense. "I don't want you to be alone with her. She was always so nasty to you, bullying you like that. And I want to make sure for myself that she's not going to write a bad review for us."

I can feel Tracy shuffle awkwardly at my mother's words. Tracy was Samantha's right hand girl in high school, so a lot of the nasty comments and not so funny pranks came from her, too.

"And that mother of hers is a real piece of work, as well. You would think she was doing me the biggest favor in the world by calling her daughter. Did I look down my nose at her last year when I had to make that special ointment for her thighs?" My mother tosses her silk scarf back over her shoulder. "I'm a firm believer, though, that people like that get what's coming to them eventually."

Luisa whimpers beside me.

"Luisa, darling, what's wrong?" my mother asks, but I put my arm around Luisa's shoulders to stop her from responding.

"Luisa is feeling a little under the weather," I say, stroking her hair.

"Oh, you poor thing," my mother says. "Do you need to take the day off?"

Luisa nods her head and wipes her eye.

"That might be a good idea," I say, seeing my opportunity. "Why don't you take Luisa home?"

"I'll ask Mr. Patterson," my mother says, referring to the handyman at the Inn. "I can start on Luisa's work."

"No!" I say, quickly taking my arm from around Luisa's shoulder. "She's actually not that sick."

"You know, I'm not feeling too good," Luisa says to me and I wave away her comment.

"You'll be fine. "

"Kate, if she says she's not well…" my mother argues.

"She's fine! We are all fine," I say, trying to hide my panic and look to Tracy for help.

"You know," Tracy hedges, "we do need someone to go and pick up those new brochures from the printers in Ridgewood."

"Right," I nod, catching her drift. "And we need them for this weekend. Shoot. I can't believe I forgot."

I try to cover my nostrils, pretending I have an itch on the top of my nose.

"Well if you need to go, I can cover things here." My mother starts to sit in the chair behind the desk.

"No!" I pull her back up. "I can't go, I have to sort out the catering for tonight, and I'm the only one who knows the menu."

"Write it down, then," my mother says.

"I haven't decided on everything yet," I explain.

"Well, I don't want to drive all the way to Ridgewood. It will take me all day to get there and back. Can't you send a courier?" she argues.

"They don't have anyone to get it here in time," I say and try to remain calm. Honestly, I ask her to do one thing, and it's like it's the end of the world.

I can tell my mother is still hesitant and I play the only card I have left. "Maybe I should just ask Viv."

I can see my mother's lips tighten. Really, I don't want to encourage it between the two of them. But, desperate times call for desperate measures.

"Honestly, I'm sure Vivienne has better things to do than go out and get brochures for our Inn," my mother argues.

"Probably, but if she knows it's important to me..." I say, but my mother is already picking up her purse.

"No, I can go and get them. No need to bother her," she says. "In fact, I was thinking that with the review it might be better to postpone our dinner tonight. Our attention should be fully focused on the Inn right now, don't you think?"

"I can honestly say my entire attention is focused on our critic," I reply.

"Good," my mother nods. "Not that I wasn't looking forward to tonight. You'll have to send my regrets to Vivienne. And Greg the Great, of course."

"Of course," I say and kiss my mother on the cheek.

I watch her leave, peering out the window until I see her car's taillights disappear from the Inn's parking lot, before letting out my breath.

"What's the deal with your mother and Vivienne?" Tracy asks as she sits behind the reception desk.

"I'm not sure how it started, but it's a mutual hate, not so carefully disguised as a tolerable friendship."

Vivienne is Greg's mother. She lives just around the corner from me, and is an up and coming interior designer. She only started working again a few years ago after Greg's father died– not that she needs to. Apparently Greg's father made all the right investments and left Vivienne a small fortune. Most of her clients are in the city, but she helped me pick out all of the furniture for the Inn. Well, I say help. We mainly disagreed about everything because my tastes run towards antiques and floral, and her taste is very contemporary and sleek. She did convince me on some heavy silver metal phones for the rooms which do look very retro.

One day, after a fight with Greg, I was unloading my story onto my mother (the one and only time, and really it's because he broke my new clipboard), it all came out. My mother hates the way Vivienne's hair is so red that it could stop cars, "but she refuses to admit she dyes it. And those god awful matching nails of hers don't help." She also hates how she walks, how she talks, and how she laughs. But most importantly, she hates that Viv tells everyone I'm the daughter she never had.

I bend my head to study one of the reservation names that the front desk clerk has illegibly written down. I love a neat and tidy appointment book, and the scrawling name is like a blemish staring up at me.

I nearly jump out of my skin as the shrill noise of the front desk bell breaks my concentration.

The shock on my face is met with a pair of studious brown eyes. His tall frame supports wide shoulders, covered by a sports coat which is open at the front to reveal a wrinkled white shirt underneath. Though his upper body is built, I can see there is a leanness to his frame, most likely due to his height. His sandy brown hair is a bit of a mess, either from the wind or it's just naturally all over the place, which emphasizes his strong cheekbones and straight nose.

He places his forearms on the ledge of the reception desk, his tall frame forced to lean over to rest on his arms. He moves the stack of business cards with my name so he can read them. He doesn't move them back into place afterwards, and I pick up the pen in front of me to stop my hands from straightening them.

"Checking in?" I ask.

"No, I'm looking for Katherine Foster," he says in an off-handed tone while his eyes take in the surrounding area.

"That's me; is there something I can help you with?"

He stands up straight and stretches his hand out to me. "I'm Detective Ben Gable. This is my partner, Donald Rice." I didn't notice the man standing behind him. Detective Rice is much shorter and has a military-style haircut; his shirt is ironed and neatly tucked into his pants. His eyes take in the reception area, looking at every corner while Detective Gable focuses on the three of us standing behind the desk.

"We got a call about a—"

"You must be here for the fire drill," I interrupt as Mr. Patterson comes out of the kitchen carrying a toolbox.

Detective Gable looks from me to Mr. Patterson and doesn't say anything.

"I have made sure everyone knows they have to stay here, until the drill is over," I say, trying to let him know where I am going with this. Mr. Patterson puts his toolbox down and takes out a screw driver, inspecting the wall plug by the front door.

"Shall I show you where we keep the fire extinguisher?" I ask and wait. Wait for him to react; wait for him to announce that we have a murdered woman upstairs and his SWAT team is waiting outside for his signal. Wait for him to straighten my business cards.

"Please," he says. "Lead the way."

Picking up my clipboard and telling myself the business cards can wait, I place a check mark on the bottom of the piece of paper. *Show detectives the body:*

check. I nod my head to Tracy and Luisa to tell them to follow me.

We reach the bottom of the staircase and I stop suddenly.

"Sorry, I just forgot something." I run back to the reception desk. I open the drawer and discretely put my inhaler in my pocket. I'm not sure how I am going to react to seeing Samantha, but I'm pretty sure passing out isn't going to help.

I also straighten the cards. Honestly, it's just one less thing to think about.

Returning to the staircase I notice a bemused look on Detective Gable's face. He was obviously watching my every move as I ran back.

Once we are at the top of the staircase, I turn to the right side and make sure they are following. When we get outside the door of Samantha's room I put my hand on the doorknob and I hesitate.

Taking a deep breath I turn around and block the doorway.

"Before we go in there, I just want you to all know that I have put my life into this Inn. My blood, sweat and tears are in every single floorboard."

Literally. I nearly lost my index finger when I tried to operate the chop saw for the wood floors. "Whatever we find in here, I can assure you, you will have our full cooperation. But, I am begging you—" I stop myself when I see the detective's raised eyebrows.

I nod sharply, turn around and insert the master key into the lock, and turn the handle.

Three

I open the door and enter the room, stopping abruptly when I see Becky standing in the sitting area with a duster in her hand. Suzanne, the emergency operator, begged my mother to give Becky, her daughter, a job at the Inn after she dropped out of high school last year. Becky's actually been doing very well and is a great help in translating Luisa's Spanish. Apparently Spanish was the only thing Becky was actually good at in school. Luisa has taken the young girl under her wing, and I know she loves bossing her around. Becky has a large set of headphones on and is bobbing her head to the music while swiping the duster back and forth over the sitting room table.

My eyes are wide with shock and I stand frozen in place, but Luisa pushes past me and grabs the duster from the girl's hand, causing her to jump.

"I told you not to use this duster on la mesa," Luisa says and inspects the wood.

"Gosh, sorry." Becky says and takes us all in, looking very nervous. "Am I in trouble? I just forgot which duster– I'll get it right next time."

"It's okay." My eyes dart around the room. It has a large sitting room as you first walk through the door, with an opening to the right leading to the bedroom. The door has been left ajar, but Becky obviously hasn't gone in there yet. At least, I hope her reaction after seeing a dead body wouldn't be to clean the coffee table.

"Who are you?" I hear Detective Gable ask Becky.

"Becky Barber, I'm the housekeeper." Becky sees Luisa's death stare and quickly amends, "*Assistant* housekeeper."

"Alright, this is really important Becky: what have you touched?" he asks her and nudges me to the side to get into the room.

"Nothing, I was just finishing dusting the room." I see the panicked look on Becky's face as she tries to figure out what she has done wrong. "But I'll do it again… properly this time. Ms. Luisa asked me to start on the sitting room."

"I say do room dos cero ocho, not dos cero *siete,*" Luisa argues.

"Sorry, I didn't get to numbers in class," Becky says and looks at me with pleading eyes. "Please don't tell my mom about this, she'll freak."

"It's okay," I say and take a step forward. "We're just having a fire drill today and this is the…

33

umm… home base. No one is supposed to be in here."

Becky looks around, taking us all in, and finally shrugs. "Okay, no problem."

I breathe a sigh of relief and turn around to Detective Gable. "She's just a young girl. She shouldn't be here," I say, silently pleading with him. I can see all the others looking at us and following the conversation.

He studies my face, his jaw tightening before he nods. "You get her out. We see what the situation is, but if it's… bad… we have a procedure we need to follow."

I nod and turn to ask Becky to leave, but she's not by the table anymore. I look around to see Becky opening the bedroom door with a pile of towels in her hand.

"I'll just put these away before I go,' she says.

"Becky, no–" I say, but it's too late.

I have never heard someone scream so loud in my entire life. It seems to go on and on, and now I am petrified by her reaction to go anywhere near the door. Detective Gable is the first to move and puts his body between Becky and the door opening. He looks over his shoulder, taking in the situation in a few short seconds, before returning his attention to Becky's face.

"Becky," he shakes her shoulders hard to get her attention. "Becky!"

She stops screaming and moves her eyes away from the door.

"Becky, this is very important. I need to know exactly what you touched."

I'm not sure Becky hears anything he says. She just keeps staring at the bedroom door as her body shakes.

I propel myself into motion and rush over to Becky, putting my arm around her. I know it's the detective's job, but he obviously can't see that Becky is in a state of shock.

"Becky, come sit down," I instruct, but the detective grabs my arm.

"No, no one can move. This whole scene could be contaminated," he looks around with a frown.

"She's going to pass out," I say, taking in Becky's stark white face and the weight of her body. She is getting heavier and heavier as she slumps against me.

"No one moves," he orders and lifts his gaze to the other detective. "We're going to need a team."

At this point I feel like I may pass out. But I also know what I have to do. I have to look. I have to know.

I lift my gaze over the Detective's shoulder and I think I might be sick. There, on the bed, is Samantha

Manning.

Her face is pale, her brown eyes open wide, her mouth slightly ajar as though she is attempting to scream but no sound is coming out. She's wearing the same red dress she wore to dinner last night and her hands are gripping the bed sheet. I can see the vivid red color of her nail polish, a stark contrast to the crisp white duvet cover that her body is resting on. Her throat– oh God, I can't even talk about it.

Just last night she was at dinner, and now…

Now she's dead.

The dinner started out fine, and by fine I mean Samantha made jokes at my expense while I laughed nervously.

I felt Vivienne squeeze my hand under the table and I really appreciated her support, especially because Greg was texting and not paying attention.

And all I can say is, thank God Mom wasn't able to come last night because she would have leaned across that table and strangled Samantha herself.

Okay, maybe a bad analogy.

Mom could never understand why I didn't stand up to Samantha in school, but I honestly didn't think it was worth the effort. The more you show them it bothers you, the more they will keep on doing it.

Though, apparently with Samantha, that reasoning didn't really work because she never did stop. Last night being the shining example.

"And then Kate had those terrible braces," she smiled and looked at me sadly. Like she felt sorry for me. But you know what, no one would have noticed the braces if she didn't point them out any chance she got. "It must have been terrible for you getting all that food stuck in them all the time."

"Hmm," I smiled, nodding my head. Two nights. That's all I had to do: put up with Samantha for two nights.

"And what's that name everyone used to call her?" Samantha asked, looking to Tracy, who seemed mortified at the conversation. I saw the argument on the tip of her tongue and I quickly intervened.

"Brace face," I offered, subtlety shaking my head at Tracy.

Two nights, how hard could two nights be?

Samantha shrieked with laughter, her chest inching closer and closer to the edge of her dress with each movement. It reminded me of a wave at high tide, coming and going just an inch closer every time. Honestly, I didn't know how she got those things in there.

Her red dress was skin tight, and without a zipper in sight I'm at a loss for how she got it on. Her shoes were at least four inches tall and her long blond hair seemed to constantly sway.

I ran my sweaty palms over my blue silk dress (I won't mention the huge stained caused by Samantha's drink when it spilled on me) and checked that the silver belt around my waist was still in place. Getting ready for last night, I had thought I looked pretty nice with my hair straightened, but Greg had just given me a quick smile and a kiss when he walked in. I thought I would at least get a "you look nice" out of him.

"Oh, it's so nice to get away like this," Samantha said, looking around the room in what I am sure she thought looked like she was reminiscing. To me it just looked like she was looking for her next prey. "New York can just wear on you, don't you think Greggy?"

Greg smiled at Samantha before going back to his phone. Samantha has always called him that… Greggy. It makes him sound like a frog. You would think he would ask her to stop. He's probably just trying to be polite, though. He's just so great like that.

"I mean, if I get one more desperate person calling me for a review," she sighed as though her life was plagued with hardship. "It's pathetic."

I attempted a sympathetic smile and swallowed the lump in my throat.

I desperately called her for a review.

"And people always think if they put something nice in my room, bring a special gift to the table, it will change my opinion," she shook her head. "I write what I want, when I want."

I had to get that basket of soap out of her room.

"Please," she put on a high pitched voice, "this means the world to me. My business depends on you."

I saw Tracy's eyes widen while she clenched the tablecloth with her fists. I looked beside me and Vivienne looked livid too.

"It seems like you have a lot of burdens on your shoulders," I said to Samantha. "That's why we are pleased you could come to relax and get away from it all."

She looked at me as though she had forgotten I was there and just shrugged.

Let's just say that was the high point of dinner and leave it at that.

When dessert was served I excused myself and found Becky in the kitchen.

"Oh dear God," I said, grabbing the young girl by her shoulders. "You need to go and get Luisa to take that basket out of Samantha Manning's room, right now!"

"The one I made with the soaps?" she asked, looking puzzled. "What's wrong with it?"

"Nothing," I said, shaking my head. "I just can't give it to her."

"I worked on those soaps all night," she complained.

"I know, I know," I said, peering through the round window on the kitchen door to make sure everyone was still eating and Tracy wasn't killing anyone. "I'll give them to someone else."

"But you told me to make the lavender ones so it would relax Miss. Manning for the review," Becky pointed out.

"Becky, I don't have time to explain. Just go and get the freaking soaps back!" I said.

Becky's eyes welled with tears but she nodded. "Okay, but please don't tell my mom you don't like them. I told her I was starting a new business and she offered to give me some start-up money."

"I love them! In fact, I will buy them for every room in the Inn," I said, desperately trying to get the girl to stop crying. "Just please go and get them from the room."

"Okay," Becky looked joyful at the prospect of so many soap orders. "I can't give you a bulk discount though, unless you give me a deposit."

"Becky!"

"Okay, okay," she said, holding up her hands.

I got back when everyone was just finishing and

Samantha stood up before I could even sit down.

"I'm tired."

She didn't even say goodnight. Just walked away from the table.

Greg and Vivienne left moments later, they both said they had to work early. Tracy and I sat at the table and neither of us knew what to say. So we shared a bottle of wine.

Sometimes wine is all the talking you need.

And I got drunk last night because I wished Samantha was dead, but at the same time I was so desperate for a good review. And now look where I am. I am never wishing for anything again.

My breathing starts to come in gasps, and between Becky and myself I am no longer sure who is supporting who.

"Oh Christ," Detective Gable says and calls the other detective over to help Becky. I stand in a state of shock, my lungs struggling to open, the oxygen unable to get down my wind pipe, and I start to see black spots appear in my vision.

My shaky hand reaches inside my jacket pocket until I can feel the cold plastic and my fingers wrap around it. I bring out my inhaler, shake it vigorously, and take a long inhale. My breathing slowly returns to normal and I reach my hand out to lean on the wall but stop before I touch it. I'm not supposed to touch anything in here.

I'm going to have to keep more inhalers on hand this week. I'll have to add it to my list tonight.

"Is everyone in here?" I hear the voice from the hallway, recognize it immediately, and try to block the doorway. My one arm still clutches my clipboard, my other traps Detective Gable in the room.

"Oh, there you are," my mother says as she enters the sitting room. "You never told me the address in Ridgewood."

My eyes dart to Tracy's face, but she looks completely dumbfounded.

"What's going on?" my mother asks, looking at Becky's limp form held upright by Luisa.

No one answers, and I swallow down the panic.

"What is everyone doing here?" she asks again, and her eyes lock in on the inhaler I have grasped in my hand. "What's wrong?"

"Nothing," I say, shaking my head. "There's a fire inspection and—"

"I'm sorry, who's *this*?" I hear the Detective's exasperated voice from behind me.

"I'm Tara Foster, Kate's mom. I own the Inn with her."

The detective moves my arm and steps in front of me, going to the suite's main door and closing it.

"Okay, everyone listen very carefully. This is a

crime scene. It has already been heavily contaminated. No one is to move an inch until the team gets here."

"Crime scene?" my mother laughs, but everyone's serious faces force her eyes to seek mine. "Kate?"

"There's been an accident," I try and explain.

"That's not an accident!" Becky finally comes to and yells. "She's been murdered!"

Not helping the situation.

"What? *Who's* been murdered?" my mother raises her voice and I wave my arms to try and quiet both of them.

"The other guests will hear you!" I frantically whisper.

"It's Samantha Manning," Tracy says.

My mother gasps.

"We really should get the team in now, Ben," Detective Rice says from beside Luisa.

"Is there absolutely no way to do this without a team?" I ask, pleading with Detective. "Or, could you maybe ask them to dress in firemen's costumes? I could just pop to the party store in the next town—"

"Are you *serious*?" he asks.

"How long has everyone known she's dead?" my mother asks, glaring at me.

"Not long," I say, trying to calm the outburst I

43

see brewing on her face.

"Did you know before asking me to pick up the brochures?" she accuses.

I avoid her eyes and cover my nose again. "I can't remember."

"I want to go home!" Becky wails from besides Luisa.

"Si, I go home now too," Luisa starts crying.

"I haven't touched anything, can I go?" Tracy asks.

"When were you going to tell me?" my mother asks. "You never let me be a part of anything!"

"Quiet!" Detective Gable yells from beside me and I jump as he rubs his forehead in exasperation. "This is insane. There is a woman in the next room who has been murdered, you have all contaminated the scene, and you're asking us to dress up as firemen while figuring everything out!"

I take in his bewildered look and can't help but frown. Honestly, if this is the worst he's seen he needs to work in the hospitality industry for a day. Last week I had to host the Christian Women's Alliance on the same weekend as the Adult Toy Tradeshow. Now *there's* a struggle.

"Okay, I know this is extremely unorthodox, but I am just asking you to see it from my point of view. You're obviously not from around here, but if you were, you would know that our town needs this Inn. It has the potential to be a big source of income, not to mention all the traffic it will bring to the surrounding businesses. If it gets out that there was a murder here, we are through. No one will step foot through that door, and everything I have been working for– everything *we* have been working for– for the last few years will have been for nothing."

I look at the hard set of Detective Gable's face, and shake my head. "You didn't know Samantha Manning, but she wasn't a very nice person–"

"God rest her soul," my mother interrupts.

"Of course," I nod. "But to be honest, I can think of more people that would want her dead than alive. She terrorized anyone she came in contact with. Having said that, I know the people in this town, and no one is capable of this, so to punish us all would be unjust. I'm not asking you not to investigate. Obviously if there is a murderer out there, I want them caught more than anyone else. I'm just asking– I'm begging you– that if there is any way to do this without broadcasting it to the world…"

Everyone's eyes are on the detective's face. He studies my face, taking it in with all its utter desperation. After what feels like an eternity of silence, he mutters something under his breath, calls

Detective Rice over to the corner of the room, and lowers his voice so we can't hear.

"You can't be serious," I hear Detective Rice say before shaking his head and letting Detective Gable continue.

"How could you not tell me?" my mother accuses from beside me. I turn to see her arms crossed and her head tilted up and away from me.

"Mom, I'm sorry. I didn't want you to worry," I say.

"No, you didn't want me to mess something up," she says, and although she's right I can't help but look annoyed.

"That's not it at all," I argue.

"I bet you would have told your precious Vivienne," my mother says, and it takes everything inside of me not to roll my eyes.

"Mother, please, can we not do this right now?"

"You always pick her side," she says, and I notice the genuine hurt in her features.

"Mom, I wouldn't have told Vivienne. I wouldn't have told anyone!" I say, and when I look at the other women in the room staring at me I quickly amend, "I mean, besides the police."

"I own the Inn too, you know; I got us the investment we needed and yet you treat me like I am a liability!"

I decide this isn't the right time to bring up the insurance policy. Or the time she set the kitchen on fire during a séance because she thought the mansion was haunted. Or the time she hired a company to set fireworks off in the back property which sent one of our oldest trees up in flames. There's actually quite a few stories involving fire, hence why I now keep a fire extinguisher in every room in the Inn.

"Honestly, can we talk about this later?" I ask with forced patience.

"Of course, I don't want to be a bother," my mother mutters.

"Okay, this is what we are going to do," Detective Gable comes back and stands beside me with his partner standing behind him shaking his head. He runs his hands through his wavy hair and now I have a better idea of why it looks so disheveled. Whatever it is they have decided, I can tell that Detective Rice doesn't like the plan. "We are all going to leave this room and not breathe a word of this to anyone."

"We are going to bring a team in—" he pauses as though he is unsure if he is capable of saying whatever is next. "We are going to bring a team in and instruct them to wear firemen's costumes. At this point the scene is compromised, and Becky has probably dusted away any prints we would have found in here, anyways. The only thing I can see working at this point is for us to dust the room and hope we come up with some DNA or trace evidence, but my gut is telling me there isn't any. We need to let everyone else know as little as possible, lull whoever did this into a false sense of security, and hope they slip up somehow while we follow any leads and investigate."

I'm at a loss for words. I never thought he would agree.

"Thank you—" I say.

"Don't thank me yet. I have a feeling this might blow up in our faces." The Detective's eyes seek out Becky's. "Not a word to anyone."

She nods and looks like she might not be able to say anything for the rest of her life.

"Her mom knows," I say, and when he turns around I explain. "She's the emergency dispatcher. We'll have to get to her quick because she's the town's biggest gossip."

"No offense," I add to Becky, but she just shrugs as if she's not hearing anything new.

"Okay, Detective Rice will go and warn her. She should still be on duty so hopefully she hasn't had a chance to tell anyone yet. If this is going to work, we can't let anyone know, or else we go public. I'll stay here and lead the team," Detective Gable instructs.

"Anything you need, I'll make sure you have it," I say.

"I still can't believe I am agreeing to this," he mutters. "We're going to need the costumes."

I nod and write it down on the bottom of my checklist: *get dozen fireman's costumes from Party City*, when my eyes light up.

"Oh! I've just remembered I have a coupon for purchases over fifty dollars."

Four

"Sit! Mommy said to sit!" I stare at the big brown eyes and count to ten. "You can do this. I know you can. Sit!"

I am standing on my front lawn out of breath, with my hair all over the place, and a blister on my heel to add insult to injury.

I plaster on a fake smile and wave to Mrs. Phelps as she drives by.

Okay, I can do this.

"Maggie, mommy said to sit!" I try and use the commanding tone I was taught, but I don't think either of us is buying it.

Maggie's tail starts wagging as she bounces from side to side.

"That's it, I'm not joking now. You come inside right now or I'm calling the humane society. They'll come and pick you up and let me tell you, you can forget about your Royal Canine diet." My words are met with a few barks.

I clench my fists in frustration and take a threatening step forward, but Maggie sees it as a never ending game and does a few laps around me—

always careful to keep out of grabbing distance–
before she resumes her stance of bouncing back and
forth.

"Naughty girl!" I yell and stamp my foot, but I'm
momentarily distracted by a black SUV pulling into
my driveway. I frown when I don't recognize the
vehicle.

The car door opens and I feel my palms start to
sweat when I see Detective Gable step out, wrinkly
shirt and all.

"Having trouble?" he asks, nodding at Maggie.

"No, just playing with Maggie," I say and shoot
the dog a severe look so she knows I'm only being
polite because we have company.

"She's beautiful, is she a mix breed?" he asks.

"No, a purebred poodle," I say with a hint of
pride in my voice. I spent a month researching
different breeds of dogs before I finally decided on
Maggie. Not only because poodles are one of the
smartest breeds, and the national dog of France (I've
always wanted to go to Paris), but because they are
very athletic and wonderful to train.

Except, I obviously got the lemon.

"Impressive," he says and snaps his fingers. I
watch, dumbfounded, as Maggie gets up and trots
over to Detective Gable, sits beside his leg, and waits
to be pet.

"How did you do that?" I ask, momentarily forgetting that I am supposed to be the expert.

"Do what?" he asks. They both look at me while he pets Maggie's head.

That traitor.

"Is something wrong?" I ask, hoping to change the subject.

I stayed at the Inn until the team of investigators arrived. True to his word, Detective Gable made sure they were all dressed in firemen's costumes, though he drew the line and refused to wear one himself. I arranged a fire drill, getting all the guests and staff to stand on the back lawn while the ambulance came to the front to take Samantha's body to the morgue. I actually felt pretty sad. I mean, not that she was ever nice to me, but to have your body removed and taken to the morgue like that, without anyone there to be sad about it, is very depressing. The detectives tried to contact her mother, but she is out of the country, and they couldn't get a hold of her. I couldn't think of anyone else to suggest they try to contact. I stood in the corner of the suite, watching as the team dusted everything. I watched as they put all her clothes in a bag, her toiletries in another: eye shadow, mascara, fifty shades of lipstick, a really pretty shade of gold nail polish and her toothbrush. They needed a separate bag for her hair products. They came out with a lot of bags labeled "evidence", and about three hours later they were gone.

"Nothing so far– it's going to take a few days for the lab to come back with anything, and we still haven't been able to reach her mother," he reaches down to pick up a ball that Maggie always keeps in her mouth. I can see it's shiny from her slobber, but I have given up trying to Lysol wipe it. As long as it stays in her mouth, which it usually does, I just try not to think about it. Detective Gable waves the ball in front of Maggie's face and gets her to stand up and wag her tail before he throws it under the tree at the corner of my lawn.

Maggie rushes over to the ball, scoops it up and runs back to him, dropping the ball at his feet. I have been trying to teach that dog catch for two weeks and I can't even get her to let me throw it.

I'm demanding a refund from the training school.

"Well, that's good. I mean not *good*–" I quickly amend. "I just thought, because you came over, something might have happened."

"No, nothing so far. There is something I have to talk to you about, though–" he says, but is interrupted by my ringing phone.

"Sorry, it could be the Inn," I say, rooting

around in my purse. Normally my phone is in the front pocket next to my package of Kleenexes but I must have just thrown it into the main pocket in my rush to get home to let Maggie out. I don't know what is happening to me today.

"Hello," I say, bringing the phone to my ear.

"Hi Honey," I hear the voice and automatically relax.

"Hi Viv, how are you?" I ask.

"Oh, not bad. Nothing a good glass of wine wouldn't cure," she laughs at her own joke which makes me smile. "The Cilans asked me to redo their living and dining room because their daughter's wedding is coming up in a few months, but they won't let me get rid of any of their old furniture. And when I say old, I'm not talking about good old, I'm talking 80's old."

"You'll convince them. You always do," I say, and watch as Detective Gable makes Maggie roll over before he will throw the ball to her again.

"Anyways, I can tell you all about it at dinner tonight," she says.

"Oh, dinner. I completely forgot," I say, biting my lip and trying to think of a good excuse to cancel.

"Am I that forgettable?" she laughs again.

"No, of course not. It's just—" I pause. I should really cancel the dinner tonight, but a part of me really wants to see Vivienne and Greg. I know I can't tell them anything about what is going on, but I don't get to see them that often. Work is really busy for Greg right now. "Is six o'clock still okay with you?"

"Absolutely, and tell your mother I look forward to one of our lovely chats," she says. Vivienne is fully aware that my mother can't stand her, and I think she enjoys watching my mother swallow her pride and be nice to her. It's actually one of the few things about Vivienne that irks me a little.

"Okay, see you then," I say, pressing the end button on my phone.

"Who was that?" Detective Gable asks, and at first I find the question a little rude. I shrug it off, though, as it *is* part of his profession to be inquisitive.

"It was my boyfriend's mother. We're all supposed to have dinner tonight at the Inn," I explain.

He nods, but doesn't say anything else about it.

"So, you wanted to talk to me about something?" I ask.

"I talked to my captain about the case, and he isn't happy with the way things are being handled."

I open my mouth to protest, but he holds up his hand.

"I convinced him that given the circumstances, and the fact we haven't found any physical evidence, we don't have a lot of options."

"And tell him your team is welcome to keep the costumes," I say, "in case you guys want to use them again."

"I didn't tell him that part, I already got an ear full without it," he says.

I feel a bit guilty at his confession because I know that if it weren't for me and my staff his whole investigation would be further along at this point.

"I'm really sorry, I honestly didn't mean to get you in any sort of trouble," I say.

He finally smiles, and it softens his sharp features. His hair is still really messy though. "When you're a detective you are always in trouble, and when you finally catch the bad guy you're lucky if you get a grunt of appreciation for your efforts."

"Oh, okay. Well, I meant what I said before, if there is anything I can do to help," I offer.

"There is. I need to stay at the Inn under the pretense of being a guest," he says.

"What? Why?"

"You've made it clear you want to keep this under wraps, which I have agreed to, honestly because I think it's the best chance we have of catching the murderer. If I'm hanging around the Inn all the time people are going to start to get suspicious, but if I am a guest just getting to know people around the town and asking casual questions, hopefully people won't catch on."

That does make sense.

"Okay, not a problem," I say, and then shake my head. "Actually, there is a problem. We are fully booked and the only room that is now available is— was— Samantha's."

"That's okay, dead people don't bother me," he says, and I wish I was as lucky as him. Standing in that room while the investigators were working, I had decided to redo the whole thing, including all the linens, to rid the room of any sense that someone might have died inside it.

"When do you want to check in?" I ask.

"I already have my suitcase in the car. I was hoping we could do it now," he says.

"I'll call Luisa and tell her to get the room ready." I pull out my cell phone again and make the call. After much reluctance on Luisa's part to go in "the room of death", I finally convince her. Of course, I had to offer her a paid vacation to do it.

"I'll just put Maggie in the house and meet you there," I say.

"I can drive you," he says. "I noticed that you walked home, so it saves you walking back."

"Oh— er— okay, thanks," I say.

I look from him, to Maggie, to the front door

and I'm not sure how to proceed.

"Do you need help?" he asks in an off-handed tone.

"No," I say.

Honestly, I run a sort-of successful Inn (minus the death today). I think I can manage to get one dog into a house.

Right, I can do this. I took the course. I read the "Bringing Out The True Potential In Your Canine" book. Twice. It's all about authority.

"Maggie," I say and feel a surge of encouragement when she turns to look at me. "Here," I point to the spot beside me.

The damn dog just blinks.

"Maggie," I say in a more threatening tone. "Here!"

She yawns and moves Detective Gable's hand with her head, asking him to pet her.

"Right," I say, stepping towards her while attempting to grab her collar.

She takes this as an indication that our previous game is back on and leaps away, doing a mad dash to the tree and back. I want to scream in frustration but instead force a laugh in the Detective's direction. "It's a game we play. It's stupid really," I say.

Honestly, this dog is going to be the death of me.

"Looks like fun," he says grinning from the dog to me. "Though we really should get back to the Inn."

"Right, of course," I say, looking around for inspiration. I take a deep breath and pick up a stick. It's my last hope. "Maggie, what's this?"

I wiggle the stick and she follows it with her eyes.

"Do you want the stick?" I say, and her tail wags energetically, which I take as a yes. "Okay, come get it!"

I run towards the front door and can hear her excited feet running behind me. I race up the steps, two at a time, and reach for the doorknob– turning it while putting my full force into opening the door. The door, however, doesn't budge, and I rebound off it like a yoyo, falling into a heap on the front steps.

Putting my hands to the ground, I gently try taking my weight off my rear end. I get a slobbery kiss on my face before Maggie takes the stick out of my hand, and runs back to the front yard.

I can hear the roaring laughter coming from Detective Gable and turn to see him bent over petting the dog. He ruffles the top of her head before coming up the walkway, up the front steps, and opening my front door.

"Here," he commands, and Maggie joyfully

prances over to him and through the doorway to sit in the front hallway, looking at him in wonderment.

"You should probably lock this," he says as he closes the door and walks back down the path.

My injured pride, and bottom end, choose not to reply to his advice as I get up off the floor and lock the door.

I dust off the specks of dirt from my clipboard, before coming around the passenger side of the black SUV.

Detective Gable is already sitting behind the steering wheel, so I open my own door. I stop and stare at the interior of his car. It is *full* of junk. There are papers scattered all over the floor. Coffee cups fill every cup holder in sight. His back seat is piled with clothes and boxes of files. I can't even bring myself to picture the trunk.

"You know, I think I'll just walk," I say.

"It will be easier if we go together. Don't you think you should be there when I check in? In case the employees have any questions?" he asks, raising one of his eyebrows.

In theory, he's right. But in actuality, I am not sure I can get into the car no matter how logical his arguments are.

"Is there a problem?" he asks, probably because I continue to hesitate.

I take a deep breath and clutch my clipboard tightly to my chest. This is the longest day of my life.

Carefully getting in so my feet don't trample on any of the papers on the floor, I put my seatbelt on and sit up straight with my elbows tucked in.

"The department is willing to reimburse you for the room," he says as he pulls out of the driveway.

"That's not necessary, Detective Gable," I say and fight to not lean to the side when the car turns.

"You should call me Ben," he says while running a yellow light at the end of the street. "It would kind of defeat the purpose of being undercover if you are referring to me as 'Detective'," he points out, and I cling to the seat as we go a little too fast over a speed bump.

"Right, sure," I say, and my hand instinctively reaches out to stop the files that he has resting on the dashboard from falling onto my lap.

"We have to instruct the employees that know what's going on to treat me the same way they would any other guest," he says.

"Absolutely," I say. I'm not even sure what I'm agreeing to right now. I can't stop looking at the drips of coffee coming out the top of one of his cups, inching their way to the cup holder ring.

"I spoke to Suzanne and she understands the importance of not talking to anyone about what she knows," he says. "She mentioned that you know a lot about the town and keep an eye on who's coming and going. I would like to sit down with you tomorrow and see if you can come up with a list for us to work with."

"Great." The drip has now gone into the cup holder.

"Would tomorrow afternoon work?" he asks.

"Sure." It's not just about the stickiness the coffee is going to leave in the cup holder. It's about the car's integrity being compromised. I mean, if a car was meant to have liquid sloshing around in it, it would be a boat.

"Is something wrong?" he asks, causing my eyes to leave the cup and look into his searching gaze.

"What? No. Nothing," I say and sigh when we make the last turn into the Inn's parking lot. "Oh good, we're here."

My seat belt is off and I am out of the car before Ben puts it in park.

Honestly, I am having a shot of tequila when I get inside, and there is nothing anyone can say to stop me.

Ben comes around to the trunk and opens it. It's worse than the inside. So much worse. Thank God I didn't see it before I got in.

"You go in first and I will bring my case in," he

says. "Just in case anyone is in the reception area."

I nod in agreement. I'm not sure my feet have ever wanted to get away from something so badly before. My blister is even telling them to hurry up.

I walk through the front door, straight to the reception desk, and collapse in the chair.

The pens are neatly lined up, just as I left them, and I lower my head to the desk in relief.

The shrill ring of the desk's bell makes me jump a few moments later, and I look up to see Ben's face.

"Checking in," he says, turning my business cards, obviously pretending to read them.

I reach up to straighten them and hand him a new guest registration form attached to a clipboard.

"Thank you for choosing the Summerside Inn. If you could just fill out the form below," I say, handing him a black ball point pen.

Ben smiles and signs the form, before putting the pen back in one of the jars. My eyes narrow slightly as I remove the pen and put it back in the jar I picked it up from. His eyes take in the labels on the jars where I have sorted them depending on the color of ink.

"So, is there a meal schedule or do we fly by the seat of our pants?" I can hear the teasing tone in his voice. Like I would ever let my pants fly.

"There is a detailed agenda in your room," I

reply. Honestly, I know that some people think I'm a little… *particular*, but I have to be. Otherwise nothing would get done and everything would fall apart.

I watch as his face becomes more serious when Mr. Patterson comes through the front door muttering about something. He hands the form back to me with his messy writing scrawled all over it.

"If you'll follow me, I'll show you to your room." Coming round the large walnut reception desk I bend to pick up his suitcase.

"What are you doing?" he asks, grabbing my arm.

The firm grip sends warm shivers up my body but I quickly ignore them. Honestly, I'm all over the place today. "I'm carrying your luggage to your room."

"I think I can manage," he says, politely refusing my assistance.

"It is the Inn's policy to show guests to their rooms, as well as carry their luggage," I argue.

"So, you can do it for the other guests," he argues. "That's too heavy for you to carry."

The argument makes me bristle with anger and I reach down and heave the suitcase off the ground. Honestly, he may have been able to tell my dog what to do, but if he thinks he is going to boss me around while he's here…

"You are supposed to be just like any other guest," I lower my voice so Mr. Patterson won't hear me. "People will think it's odd if I don't carry it for you."

Ben looks around the room before frowning, "What people?"

Okay, so there isn't anyone around right now, but you never know what could happen. I mean, did I expect to have a dead body in my Inn this morning or be helping an undercover detective solve the crime while he stays at the Inn? No. But I'm adapting. Honestly, some people are so inflexible.

The bag is heavy, but I manage it, and I don't appreciate his lack of confidence in my abilities. Policy is policy, and I am nothing if not a stickler for the rules.

"See?" I say with a forced smile on my face. "Now if you will just follow me."

I give it my best effort to not strain my walk from the heavy load in my hands, but I can feel my balance is slightly off. Ignoring Ben's observance of my struggle, I lead him out of the reception area.

"The library is across the hall, and through those double doors is the morning room and dining room," I say, pointing to the large French doors that are closed while the staff prepare for dinner. "The lounge's entrance is tucked behind the staircase, which has access to the back porch and gardens."

I stop at the oak staircase to make sure he has had a moment to process where everything is, though my arm holding the suitcase screams in protest, willing me to continue up the staircase. What does he have in this thing, bricks?

I watch as Ben observes the hand carved woodwork on the walls, which cost us a small fortune to restore. The practical, yet inviting fabrics on the arm chairs in the hallway were my personal choice and I admire the soft rose-patterned fabric.

Ben finally turns to look at me and I see the impressed look on his face.

"I didn't really have time to appreciate it earlier, but you did a great job restoring this place. I used to drive past it sometimes on my way into the city. I'm just amazed you got someone to agree to do it," he says.

"You just have to know how to ask nicely," I say, "and it only took three years to accomplish. In fact, I had a ten year plan for it, so I'm actually ahead of schedule."

"I'm sure you can be very persuasive," he says, looking at me from the corner of his eye.

"Hard work, dedication, and a little persistent nagging," I lightly joke.

The low rumble of his laugh makes me aware

that I have somehow become relaxed in his presence and I quickly straighten my back. It's not very professional to stand in the hall like this.

Seeming to notice my withdrawal, Ben indicates the stairs. "Ladies first."

I start up the stairs, lugging the heavy suitcase at my side, but my hand encounters a nail head sticking out on the banister rail and I suddenly stop. Making a mental note to get the Mr. Patterson to fix it, I start up the stairs again, but, momentarily distracted, I forget the heavy weight of the suitcase. The edge of the bag catches on the step's edge, and the force causes me to fall forwards. Before my face hits the step, though, I'm suddenly halted by a strong arm wrapped around my middle.

"Didn't your mother ever tell you not to stop suddenly on stairs," Ben lightly admonishes. The feel of his iron hard body against my back is reassuring, and for a guy that is so disheveled he smells like fresh soap.

"There's a nail head sticking out on the banister," I explain, my eyes seeking out the dark silver mark.

"Hmm..." Ben nods, looking at where my fingers are touching the banister. "In any case, I better take my suitcase the rest of the way. I don't want you accidently falling again and crushing my stuff," he jokes.

I'm not laughing as I lift my chin in the air and stride up the stairs. Crushing his stuff... if anything broke it would have been *my* neck from his rock collection in that case.

"This is your room," I say, stopping outside the first door on the right. Obviously he knows where the room is, but I've come this far with the pretense and it seems only right to finish it properly. "Your agenda is on the side table and dinner is in a few hours." I extend my hand to give Ben the key, his fingers grazing my outstretched palm.

"Thank you, Ms. Foster. You've been a very gracious guide," he says. His touch is doing irregular things to my pulse. Which is silly. Obviously I'm not thinking straight today.

"We hope you enjoy your stay Detec– Mr. Gable. Let us know if you need anything else."

"Will do," he says, smiling.

I make a note on my clipboard on the way back down the stairs to make sure Luisa is in charge of the guest in the "room of death".

I also make a note for her to iron his shirts while he's at dinner.

Five

Okay, I need to calm down. I need to take a deep breath and calm down. There are six hours left in the day; what could possibly go wrong in six hours?

You know what, forget I asked.

I blame my inhaler. I haven't had this much corticosteroid in my system since I tried to do the track and field meet in grade six. That day didn't go very well either.

Greg and Vivienne have already arrived and they're waiting for me in the dining room. I changed into one of the dresses I keep at the Inn for the evenings I don't manage to make it home before dinner. The black cocktail dress hugs my figure, but the high neckline and hem that comes to my knees give it a sophisticated, if not a bit reserved, look. Just the way I like it.

Becky's gone to my house to walk Maggie, and I hope she has better luck with her than I did.

I enter the dining room and shake my head when I see both Vivienne and Greg on their cellphones. The two of them are workaholics. Greg's a financial advisor for the Bank of America and is constantly on the phone, checking his mail, or talking to clients. It's actually kind of annoying, as I will be in the middle of a conversation with him, and the minute his phone rings he reaches for it like it's the last chocolate chip cookie. One time I hid it for the whole afternoon and I honestly thought Greg was going to go mental. I couldn't even enjoy the quiet because he was ripping his place apart looking for it. He was actually pretty mad about that for a while.

And Vivienne's business seems to be getting more and more glowing reviews, which means she is pretty busy most of the time, as well. I actually have no idea how she did it. It just seems like one day I woke up and she was this new famous designer. I asked her how she got so many great reviews, but she wouldn't tell me. Like I was somehow going to steal all her glory, or she wouldn't be the most famous person in town anymore.

Which is crazy. Everyone knows the most famous person is Whitey, our town's ghost.

Not that Greg and Vivienne really live in our town anymore. The two of them go back and forth to New York so much that Greg has a place here and one in Manhattan; but he is almost always in the city.

He's wearing his black suit tonight— he always wears a suit when he comes to the Inn for dinner; he says it gives the illusion to other guests that there is a distinguished quality to the place. At which point I always correct him, arguing it's not an illusion. He then brushes away the argument as though I'm not seeing what he meant. It's our couple banter.

His hair is neatly combed to the side with gel, making it glisten. The severe style plays up his classic Greek features, making him strikingly handsome—which I know is precisely why he styles it that way. Greg spends more time on his hair than I do, not that I mind. I mean, perfection obviously takes the time it needs to take. Though, sometimes an hour does seem a bit excessive.

Greg gets his good looks from Vivienne, who, as she gets older, seems to get more beautiful. She celebrated her sixtieth birthday last year and she still doesn't look a day over forty-five. Her red hair is set off tonight with her gold dress, and her ever present matching red nails.

"Hello, you two," I say, sliding into the seat across from Greg.

"One second honey, I'm just sending an email," he says, his fingers flying over the phone's little keyboard.

"I think I might have finally convinced the Cilans to part with their furniture, but the wife is adamant about this god awful chaise," Vivienne says, as she too types away on her phone.

I sit for a few moments in silence, watching them both engrossed in their tasks, and feel a little bored. I mean, I kept the plans for dinner tonight so I could get my mind off of everything; not to sit here and watch them send emails all night.

"Right," Greg starts to put his phone down but it beeps. He looks at the screen, shaking his head, but thankfully places it on the table to look at me and smile. He has such great teeth. "How's your day?"

"Well, not great actually," I say as Vivienne puts her phone away in her purse.

"Luisa giving you a hard time again?" Vivienne asks sympathetically. Luisa, unfortunately, is on "Team Mother" and has never been friendly to Vivienne.

"No, just busy," I say.

"Oh, good! You didn't start without me," my mother says as she walks into the dining room. She's wearing a long purple sequined gown that makes her look like a mermaid. The silver head wrap isn't doing her any favors, either.

"Tara, darling. I was worried you weren't going to be able to join us," Vivienne says, placing her hand on my mother's fingers. I can see my mother staring at Viv's nails but thankfully she doesn't say anything.

"You know I wouldn't miss dinner with my three favorite people for the world," my mother's sing song voice sounds forced.

"And what a special outfit you have on!" Vivienne smiles. "What designer is that?"

"It's vintage," my mother says. "Something I just threw on."

Vivienne smiles again before lifting up the menu to block her face.

My mother turns to me and tries to smile, but it doesn't reach her eyes.

"Mom, I forgot to tell you that dinner wasn't cancelled—" I begin but my mother waves away the rest of my sentence.

"Oh, not a problem. Luckily Luisa mentioned to me an hour or so ago that our names were still down on the reservation list tonight," she says. "It must have just slipped your mind."

I smile at her for not making a scene and pick up my own menu.

"Though a lot of things seem to be slipping your mind today," she says, and my eyes stop reading.

"Mom…" I smile and move my eyes to Greg and Vivienne to remind her we are not alone.

"No, you've had a busy day," she pats my hand and lifts up her own menu. "Though you seem to have the time to fill everyone else in on what's going on."

Luckily, our waiter Lucas, chooses this moment

to come to our table to ask if we would like any wine.

My mother orders a bottle of red, probably because she knows Vivienne hates it, and continues to read her menu.

"Kate, is that woman who's reviewing the Inn coming to the dining room tonight?" Lucas asks, and my hand freezes on my glass. "Only, she was supposed to be here at six and a couple are waiting for her table."

"No, she won't be coming for dinner," I say and lift my gaze to the others at the table. "She's umm... gone home."

"What?" Greg says, lifting his napkin from his lap and placing it on the table. "What do you mean Samantha left?"

"Something came up," I say and try to stop the panic rising from my chest. I'm at my maximum dose of inhalations today. "She had to go back to New York I think."

"But– what about the review?" he asks, and I can't help but feel better at his outraged tone. He's always looking out for me. He's so great.

"I'm sure they will send someone else," I say. That is, if we are still open for business after the investigation.

Greg shakes his head and picks up his ringing phone. "Excuse me, I have to take this," he says, getting up and walking into the main hall.

Vivienne's phone rings from inside her purse and after she sees the caller id she looks at me, "Sorry honey, this is Mrs. Cilan. I'll be right back."

I tell Lucas to hold off on our dinner orders for a minute, and when I see him begin to interact with another couple I turn to my mother. "Do you think they suspect anything?" I ask.

"Not a thing," she reassures me. "In fact, it startles me what a good liar you seem to becoming."

"Mother, please," I beg and lean towards her. "I'm sorry I didn't tell you about Samantha and about dinner, but I have honestly had the worst day of my life so could you please just cut me a *little* slack?"

She looks at my face before sighing. "You're right. I'm sorry. That woman just makes me crazy! She knew full well this was polyester before she asked who made it."

I choose not to comment in case it upsets our new found truce.

"They're coming back," I say as Greg and Vivienne both re-enter the dining room.

"I'm so sorry honey, but I have to run. Mrs. Cilan has decided to let go of all the furniture, but she insists we get it out tonight," she comes around the table to kiss me on the cheek. "We will try this again, next week perhaps?"

"Of course," I say, and see my mother visibly relax. Well, at least I won't have to be a referee between the two of them for the rest of the night. Greg thinks we should let the two of them sort it out themselves, but he doesn't know that if I let that happen one of them would end up killing the other. And quite frankly, I've already had to deal with too many dead bodies today.

"I have to run too, I'm afraid," he says, coming to kiss me on the other cheek.

"What? Why?"

"One of our clients insists on being briefed tomorrow morning about some of his new holdings, and I have to get everything together for it tonight," he says apologetically.

"Oh, okay."

"I'll make it up to you," he says before kissing my mother on the cheek. "Nice seeing you, Tara."

I smile at him as he leaves the dining room.

Well, that's disappointing. Though he did say he would make it up to me, which is nice. Trouble is, he says that an awful lot and I'm not sure if he ever does. But obviously work can't be helped. He's successful and needs to dedicate a lot of time to his clients. They all think he's great as well.

"Well, kiddo. It's just you and me again," my mother says, then takes a gulp of her red wine. I nod absently as I notice Ben come through the door of the dining room.

He's changed into a pair of beige dress pants with a shirt and tie for dinner. The shirt is actually ironed, which I suspect might be Luisa's doing, but the tie he's wearing sits loose around his collar like he didn't bother to push it up all the way. I'm going to be staring at that for the entire evening, I know it.

"Hello ladies," he says as he approaches our table.

"Mr. Gable, so nice to see you," my mother says, standing up and kissing his cheek. I saw the two of them talking on the back lawn for an hour or so this afternoon and from the smile on my mother's face I can see he charmed the pants off her.

First he charms my dog. Now my mother... what's next?

"Tara, didn't I tell you to call me Ben?" he winks at her. She laughs at this before taking her seat.

"Don't let me disturb you," he says, taking a step backwards.

"Please join us," my mother says, and I clamp my teeth down in frustration.

Okay, it's not like I have anything personal against the guy. In fact, I will even admit– though reluctantly– that he helped me a lot today. You know with the costumes, and not announcing there had been a murder. But, even so, he's just so…

It took everything inside of me to not go out to his car and clean up the coffee drops. It's all I could think about all afternoon. Well, besides the dead body of course.

All I am asking is for everyone to respect the boundaries. I will help him with the investigation in any way I possibly can, and he will stop moving my business cards.

"I really shouldn't," he says, then lowers his voice, "I don't want anyone to get suspicious."

"You're probably right—" I begin.

"Oh nonsense," my mother cuts me off and waves away his objections. "We invite guests of the Inn to our table all the time, don't we Kate?"

I nod slightly and put a false smile on my face.

"Well, if you're sure…" he says, pulling out the seat in front of him. "I actually thought I might be too late for dinner. I saw some guests leaving just as I was coming in."

"That must have been Vivienne and Greg the Great," my mother says and leans forward. "They got called into work or something. Their loss, our gain."

Ben smiles and looks from me to my mother, "Greg the Great?"

"My boyfriend," I explain. "It's my mother's

silly nickname for him."

"Don't look at me," my mother laughs, "it's all Kate's doing. Anytime I ever ask her anything about Greg her response is 'he's great'. Whether he's getting his hair cut or trading stocks, he does everything 'great'."

"I do not say that," I argue.

I don't.

Okay, maybe I have said it on the odd occasion.

But, it's true. He is great.

"And Vivienne's the one you were telling me about, Tara?" he asks, and I have to tamper down my anger when I look at my mom.

"Mother."

"I didn't say anything bad," she puts up her arms in defense. "At least, I didn't say anything that wasn't true."

I look to get Lucas' attention and call him over to take our dinner orders.

I also order a huge glass of wine.

My mom and Ben have a conversation back and forth throughout dinner; he asks questions about the town and the construction of the Inn, and my mother tells him all the latest town gossip. They seem to have forgotten that I am even at the table.

Which is fine. In fact, it's better this way.

The less I talk, the more I can drink.

And I'm really not sure what my mother is doing. I mean, she's obviously flirting with him, but Ben is half her age.

Not that there is anything *wrong* with that. He just doesn't strike me as the type who would go for an older woman.

He seems like he likes adventure, staying active.

Though, my mother is more adventurous than most people I know. She also does yoga every day and nature hikes.

But still. The two of them can't see each other. It's... It's...

Against the Inn's policy! That's right, I forgot. There is a section in the employee handbook that says staff can't date.

Except, we had to make an exception for Mr. Patterson and Luisa because she thinks they might end up getting married if he ever asks her out.

Also, we had to let Becky date the guy who mows the Inn's lawn because, as she puts it "It's totally uncool to put limitations on true love".

But, this is definitely crossing the line.

Okay, so Ben's not *technically* an employee, but really isn't he an employee of us all? He works for the state, and my taxes pay his wages.

So that's it, it's against the rules.

Except, I can't phrase it like that to my mother

or it will make her want to date him more.

He looks around to make sure he's not being overheard before he leans in towards my mother.

"What did you know about Samantha Manning, Tara?" he asks.

"She was in my year at school, so Mom didn't know her that much," I interrupt, reminding them that I am at the table too. The last thing I need today is my mother going off on a tangent about–

"Samantha Manning was a bitch," she says.

Okay, so tangent it is.

"Mom," I say in a warning tone.

"I'm sorry honey, you know I don't like to speak ill of the dead, or the living for that matter– except for a select few," she amends. "But that woman tortured my daughter in school."

My face turns red and I shoot my mother a glance pleading with her to stop.

"What?" she asks me. "She did."

"Mom, Detec– er– Ben doesn't need to hear about this right now," I argue.

Especially when he is looking for a motive as to why someone would kill Samantha.

"I'm just telling Ben what I know about her, and that is that she was a terrible person. Kate pretends she didn't care, but she used to come home crying all the time."

Lovely, could this possibly get any worse?

"They used to wait for her outside of the library and steal her books to drop them in the mud."

"They?" Ben asks, studying me from the corner of his eye.

"Samantha and Tracy. Though Tracy isn't like that anymore," I add.

Oh God, I don't want to make Tracy a possible suspect as well.

"Yes, Tracy apologized a long time ago. She's actually a very sweet girl who just got mixed up with the wrong friends," my mother acknowledges.

My mom and I have become very close to Tracy over the past few years. When she found out we were renovating the Inn she asked to be in charge of the spa section, something we hadn't even considered adding at the time. Anyways, she talked us round to it and oversaw all the construction for that area, completely free of charge for the year, while she still worked another job, in the hopes that she would be allowed to come and work here when we opened.

"My father loved this old place," Ben says as dessert is served. "He would have loved to see it restored like this."

"Did he pass away?" my mother asks.

"About ten years ago," Ben says and looks at me. "You should be really proud of what you've accomplished here."

"Thank you," I say and can't help but be genuine. It's always so nice when someone appreciates the details that went into making the Inn what it is today.

"Kate's loved this old place since the time she could walk. Her father used to take her here as a child," my mother smiles at Ben.

"Did your father get to see it restored?" Ben asks.

"No, he left when I was six," I say and push my chair back. "I'm sorry, but it's been a very busy day for me, and I have an early morning tomorrow."

"Of course," Ben says, picking up his napkin from his lap and also standing. My mother follows suit and I have no choice but to walk to the front hallway with them. I go around the reception desk and lean over to get my purse when I hear my mother whisper to Ben.

"Sorry, her father is always a touchy subject," she explains, and I look up to see Ben shaking his head as though her apology is unnecessary.

"I'll see you in the morning, mother," I say and walk up beside her to lay a kiss on her cheek.

"I'd like to get together, if possible, tomorrow afternoon," Ben says to me. "I need that list you have of the people that were in town last night."

"Of course," I say. "Is one o'clock okay?"

"That's fine."

I say goodnight again and open the door to make the short walk home. And that dog better be on her best behavior when I get there or she's sleeping outside.

Six

Today is a new day. I scrub my hair and body in the shower until I am certain there is not a trace left of the disastrous day before. I have my toast and coffee while reading the newspaper in my sunny kitchen. I tilt my head at my suits in my neatly lined closet and decide on the ash grey. I even put on my hounds tooth blouse, which is usually a print I save for the weekend. But, I deserve to have a treat today.

I have compiled a list for Detective Gable of the people that have been staying at the Inn for the past few weeks, as well as anyone I know of that may be visiting a relative in town. It's not an extremely long list. Our town's population is just over five thousand, mainly retired people or young families who don't travel much. The town was founded in 1786, and we pride ourselves on maintaining a tight knit community. About five years ago, when I applied for all the permits so the Inn could start construction, I asked the mayor if I could be in charge of a "guest book" for the town. Anyone who is coming or going, besides those just driving through, is asked to stop at the Inn and sign the book. At first it was met with a lot of eye rolling, but after a while everyone seemed to embrace it– saying it added further charm to our little town.

Now the book is a bit of a tourist attraction. And let me tell you, if someone doesn't sign that book, everyone knows. It's the first thing people ask when their guests arrive, and if they haven't stopped at the Inn they have to by the end of the day. Mrs. Phelps brought her nephew in last month by the ear and wouldn't let go until he signed in.

I love our town.

On my drive to work I make sure my portable coffee mug is firmly in place in the cup holder with the top securely on. Just as it should be.

Stepping out of my car, I collect my purse, jacket, and clipboard off the passenger seat and lift my face to the refreshing breeze. I can smell the fresh water from the lake and feel all the chaos of the previous day melt away. Today is going to be a better day.

I enter the front door and see Tracy standing behind the reception desk.

"Hi Tracy," I say and come to stand behind the desk, hanging my coat and purse up on the rack.

"Hi, Kate. We didn't expect you this early," she says, looking at her watch. "I have an early morning facial booked or I wouldn't be here myself."

"Just thought I would get a head start on things. I didn't manage to get a lot of paperwork done yesterday," I say.

"No, I guess not. Have they found anything yet?" she's asks.

"Not that I know of. They hadn't as of last night."

"It's just so creepy," she says. "I was tossing and turning all night, and Tim kept asking me what was wrong, but I obviously couldn't tell him."

I nod and put my hand on her arm in a show of support.

"I mean, you don't think anyone we know did this, *do you*?" she asks and darts her eyes around as though the killer could jump out at us any minute.

"Absolutely not," I say. "Come on Tracy, do you honestly think anyone from Summerside is capable of *murder*? It took us two years and five town meetings to agree to send that letter to Hartford politely asking them to put us on their surrounding areas map. We're not the most confrontational people."

"I know, you're right," she says. "But then, who did it?"

"I don't know," I say, shaking my head. "I went through our guest book last night and can't think of a single person that is capable of this."

Her eyes light up and she snaps her fingers. "Unless they didn't sign in," Tracy says, as though she has solved the case.

"That's what I figured too," I say. Which makes sense. If I was going to kill someone I'm not sure I would stop at the local Inn and sign my name on the guest registry. I mean, they killed someone, obviously they don't have a lot of respect for the rules.

The phone rings and Tracy stands up. "I'll let you get that. I have to go make an eighty year old look like she's sixty," she winks before walking down the hall to the newly expanded spa.

"Summerside Inn, Kate Foster speaking," I answer.

"Oh good, Ms. Foster. It's Glenn from Regal Insurance."

I scowl as I take my seat behind the desk. This shyster again. If he's calling to say my premium has increased I'm definitely cancelling. I don't care how much the penalty is, there is spite involved now.

"What can I help you with?" I ask.

"I was speaking to your mother yesterday, about your situation there," he says, and my whole body goes tense.

"What– er–situation?" I ask.

There is no way my mother would have told this

man about Samantha's body.

She knows she's not allowed to talk to anyone about it.

She knows I would be furious.

"About the murder–"

I'm going to kill her.

"Okay!" I say, cutting him off and looking around to make sure no one can overhear our conversation.

"Your mother was inquiring about your insurance policy, to see if the room would be covered in the event you wanted to redecorate it?"

Honestly, I will ask my mom to do something: sign some tax forms, send a check to the gas company, order the meat from the butchers– and she still won't have done it weeks later. I casually mention to her yesterday that we *might* want to consider redoing the room at *some point,* and she goes and calls the insurance company that minute!

"Unfortunately, because there wasn't any actual physical damage to the room, you won't be covered," he says in a tone that I'm sure he hopes is apologetic, but it just sounds condescending.

"Of course we're not," I say. There are two things I actual *hate* in this world. Insurance men and the phone company. With the amount I pay in premiums, I'm pretty sure I could buy a whole other

EMILY HARPER

Inn. I'm covered from shark bites for Christ sake, but a woman dies in a room and I want to change the linens and they won't give me a penny.

I hear footsteps coming down the stairs and peek around the corner to see Detective Gable sauntering down.

My eyes widen and I quickly whip my head back around the corner. I can't let Ben know my mother talked to the insurance company.

"Well, thank you for calling," I say and try to look relaxed as Ben comes over to the desk and leans his arms on it. I'm about to hang up the phone but Glenn is still talking.

"I did want you to know I have sent the paperwork over for you and your mother to sign, before I can release the life insurance check."

"The—" I look at Ben, who is looking around the reception area, obviously waiting for me to get off the phone. "The what?"

"The life insurance claim. You're covered when a death occurs on your premise— in the event the death causes a problem with your business or causes unforeseen damage," he says. "Your mother added it to your policy last year."

My hand is shaking and I try and swallow the huge lump in my throat. "She did that?"

"The coverage is for one hundred thousand

90

dollars, so obviously it is going to take a little time to get everything sorted. You could use some of those funds, if you would like, to redecorate the room," he suggests.

"Yes, we'll do that," I say. "I'm sorry there's just a guest at the front desk. Can I call you back a little later?"

"Absolutely," he says. "Though maybe it would be best if I come down there and walk you through everything in person."

"No!" I say, nearly jumping out of my seat. Ben turns to look at me, studying my face, and I attempt to smile at him. "Things are very busy here at the moment. Maybe we could set up a time in the next few weeks?"

"Sure, just let me know what works."

I say goodbye and slowly replace the receiver.

This is not good. This is *really* not good.

If the police find out that we took out an insurance policy when we are on the brink of bankruptcy...

And then Samantha shows up dead...

Okay, I am going to have to buy my inhalers in bulk from now on.

"Everything okay?" Ben asks, still studying me.

"Absolutely!" I try to sound normal but I can hear the strain in my voice.

Why would my mother do this? Why would she take out an insurance policy in the event that a guest dies?

Having said that, she did get shark coverage.

But, why wouldn't she mention it to me?

"I... umm... I just have to pop out for a minute," I say to Ben before turning around to grab my purse and coat.

"Is something wrong? You're a bit pale and your face is twitching," he says.

"No it's not," I wave away his concerns. "I just have something in my eye."

"Do you want me to drive you?" he asks.

"No!" I yell and have to remind myself to calm down. "No, thank you. I won't be long and I'm sure you have some investigating to do..."

"We are still good for this afternoon?" he asks, and I can tell his suspicions have been peaked at my behavior.

"Absolutely. One o'clock. It's on my checklist," I nod. I stand, with my purse and clipboard plastered against my body, and wait for him to move out of my way.

He eventually moves to the side and I can feel his penetrating eyes follow me all the way to my vehicle.

Once I am inside, and have pulled out of the

parking lot, I fish my phone from my purse and frantically dial my mother.

"Darling," my mother's sing song voice greets me.

"Mom, I'm coming over," I say.

"Alright," she says. "Is anything wrong?"

Of course something's wrong. *Everything* is wrong. My mother might just have made us the lead suspects in a murder investigation. And I'm talking on my cellphone while driving without using my handsfree– what's *happening* to me?

"I'll be there in five minutes."

Every time I walk into my mother's house I feel like I need to go back onto the front porch and check I have the right address. My mother changes her décor like I clean my apartment (on Wednesday, Saturdays and sometimes again on Sunday if things get crazy when I'm baking on Saturday).

Today she's got a bright blue velour couch with red and gold arm chairs sitting across from the fireplace. There are sheer red scarves covering the lamps to give off a warm glow, and I make a note on my clipboard: *make sure I check the fire extinguishers in Mom's house.*

"Kate, is that you?" she calls from the kitchen, and I make my way into the room to see her standing over a pot on the stove, watching something boil.

"Oh god, what's that smell?" I ask, putting my hand to my face. It smells like an orange has been left in the hot sun for days.

"Mr. Patterson's arthritis is bothering him again, so I told him I would make a special ointment," she says, stirring the liquid.

I make another note on my clipboard: *give Mr. Patterson the next few days off. Also, buy him a scented candle.*

"Mom, the insurance company called this morning," I say.

My mother's hand stills mid-stir before she flicks her hair over her shoulder and continues.

"Really, what did they say?"

"I think the better question is, *what did you tell them?*" I say, coming to stand beside her at the sink.

"Nothing." My mother stops and looks at me. "I just had to ask Glenn a quick question."

"Mom," I reach across the stove and place my hand on top of hers, "it's alright. I know you didn't mean anything by it, but I need to know exactly what you told him."

"Er..." Mom starts fiddling with her hair. "I'd rather not."

"Mom, I have a right to know."

"Really, Kate it's nothing." She looks around

the kitchen for a distraction.

"If it's nothing then why can't you tell me?"

There is a strained look on her face. She bites her lip and avoids my eyes. "Well... the truth is, I am not sure you would *approve*."

I wouldn't approve? Honestly, I know I can be a little uptight sometimes, but it's not like I go around judging people all the time. Well, at least I don't say it out loud.

I mean, she's my mother. I would try and understand anything she told me. And it's not like she—

She wouldn't have—

I look at my mother's flushed face and notice her hands are shaking ever so slightly.

Oh God, she did it. I never thought I would believe it, but at this very moment I am standing in my mother's kitchen and I honestly believe she did it. She killed Samantha Manning

My heart races with implications: she'll be arrested; she'll go to jail. My mother would never survive jail; she has the windows open in December.

I know she did this for me, she knows how much I wanted the Inn to succeed, and how it's been struggling lately. But to *murder* someone...

And it suddenly hits me— she doesn't want to tell me in case they try and make me testify at the trial.

Well, they can forget it. If they think I would testify against my own mother they have another thing coming. I'm going to get her the best lawyers money can buy (I wonder if the insurance company will still give us that money if Mom murdered the victim, because we'll need it for the defense.)

"Mom, we are not leaving this kitchen until I know *exactly* what we are dealing with." I take a sip of what looks like a cappuccino sitting on her kitchen counter, but turns out to be the strongest coffee I have ever tasted. My eyes water as I try to catch my breath in a fit of coughs.

Once I have regained control I take a deep breath, "I can handle it."

"Really Kate, you're making such a fuss over nothing. Tracy and I are just trying to make a little money for the Inn, just something to keep us going for a while."

Oh God, Tracy's in on it too. That's why she was there this morning, asking me all those questions. She wanted to see what I knew.

"And Patricia from down the lane made a fortune last year the exact same way, but she's planning to do it again this year– so inconsiderate, that woman." Mom takes a sip of her coffee.

Not Mr. Flatt! Patricia swore he died in his sleep. I went to the funeral!

"So we decided to do it ourselves, it actually wasn't that hard–"

I'm definitely going to have to plead the fifth.

"We can do it to all the guests!"

"Oh my god!" I cry and collapse into the nearest chair. "Mother, don't you see what you've *done?*"

"Honestly, I thought you'd be pleased," she says with a downcast look.

"How could you possibly think I would be pleased that you *murdered* someone?" I ask, throwing my arms in the air.

"*Murdered someone?*" she frowns. "What are you talking about?"

"I'm talking about you and Tracy killing Samantha Manning for the insurance money," I accuse.

"Tracy and I…" my mother stops and bursts out laughing.

Oh God, she's deranged. I always knew something was off about her, I even did an at-home DNA test when I was thirteen just to be sure we were related. But this… I can honestly say in a million years… I never expected this.

"You think Tracy and I killed Samantha?" she wipes a tear of laughter from her eye.

"You just admitted it to me!"

My mother shakes her head and puts her hand

on my arm. "Tracy and I are going to be doing Botox at the spa. That's what I called the insurance company about. I wanted to make sure we would be covered."

At my perplexed look my mom leans forward, "Botox is where you inject fat into different areas of your body to... freshen things up a bit."

"I know what Botox is, Mother!"

"Well, we heard on Oprah that people can make a fortune having these parties– we could even do the gardens if we get enough clientele!"

"So, you are going to be doing Botox... at the Summerside Inn?" I can't believe this. "Who will be doing the injections?"

"Tracy and I," she says smiling, "that's the best part! I went to the city on the weekend to learn how to do it myself, and to pick up the... er... *fat.*"

"Wait- you're injecting these clients *yourself*?"

"Oh yes, we save quite a bit of money doing it ourselves. And now I can teach Tracy- it's all on the up and up. I just had to take a quick course over the weekend and now I'm certified- would you like to see my card?" Mom excitedly reaches for her purse.

"No, that's alright, thanks." This is way too much for a Thursday morning.

I'm not sure what actually bothers me more: the fact my mother is injecting our (supposed to be) exclusive clientele with someone's leftover fat, or the fact that I wasn't even consulted. I mean, I have a suggestion box in the staff room for this exact purpose. No one ever respects my system.

"But if that's what you called the insurance company for, why did you tell him about Samantha?" I ask.

"Oh that, I just mentioned it because I was going to surprise you and redecorate the room."

"Mother, do you not understand that the whole investigation is being kept under wraps because no one is supposed to know about Samantha's murder?" I ask in exasperation.

"Oh, Glenn won't tell anyone! Insurance people are like lawyers, they have a *code*."

"Actually, they aren't like lawyers at all," I say, shaking my head.

"Besides, he's in New York. People get murdered there every day; it didn't even faze him." My mother brushes the argument aside and leans forward. "So what do you think?"

"About what?" I ask.

"The Botox!" my mother says.

"I don't know, I can't even think about it right now," I get up from the chair. "There's something else. Did you add to our insurance policy that if a guest dies while they are staying at our Inn we can claim life insurance?"

"I'm not sure, Glenn would know. He did the paperwork for me."

I stand up and pick up my clipboard from the table.

"I have to get back to the Inn. Maybe you should take the day off and finish Mr. Patterson's ointment," I say.

"This will be done in a few hours. I'll pop by for a cup of tea this afternoon, shall I?"

I nod and turn to leave. At this point, I don't even have the energy to argue.

And I'm definitely not telling my mother any more about the insurance money until I can figure out what to do. Knowing her, she'll just spend it all on needles and extra fat.

Seven

Sitting across from Ben in the staff room, I inspect his face while he reads the guest book, wondering what he knows and what he suspects. He will find out about the insurance policy eventually, but the question is whether I tell him, or let his team tell him.

If I tell him it might alleviate how bad it looks. I can explain how flighty my mother is, and the fact that she didn't even know what she was signing, so there is no way we could have planned it. But then, telling him might make me look guilty. Like I'm bringing it up because I *know* it looks bad.

"You are a really detail-oriented person," Ben says, and I can see from his eyes that he is impressed with my list.

I smile. I love a well-organized list.

"There doesn't seem to be anyone that has come or gone within the time frame that would look suspicious, besides the victim herself. Which means one of two things," he says, tapping his pen on the desk.

"Which is?" I prompt.

"Either the killer didn't sign your guest book and

got by your town's neighborhood watch," he pauses. "Or the killer is someone that lives here."

"No, I can't believe that," I adamantly shake my head. "I grew up in this town. I *know* these people, and they're not killers."

"You would be surprised what people are capable of in a moment of desperation," he says.

This is true. I mean, I feel like I've been at the brink of killing people (mainly my mother) in moments of desperation. But I didn't. Just because you want to do something doesn't mean you are actually capable of it.

I shake my head, "No, I just can't accept that."

He raises his eyebrows but doesn't say any more. "Tracy and her husband went out of town two weeks ago. Do you know where they went?"

"To New York; Soho I think," I say. "I can check to be sure. They got some tickets from Greg's company for a party there at an art gallery. Greg and I couldn't go."

I was actually really looking forward to going away that weekend, but Greg had to work in the end. His big client, Silverman's Mines, was coming into town and he had to get their signatures on some big deal. He did say he was going to make it up to me, though.

"And your mother was out of town last

weekend," he looks at the list again. "Where did she go?"

I try to keep my face as neutral as possible. "Into the city. She went for a shopping trip," I say. I just can't get into the Botox right now.

He just nods his head again.

"Shouldn't we be focused on who came *into* town?" I ask.

"Nothing is completely cut and dry in a murder investigation. It's just good to cover all bases. You never know what will be significant."

"Well, you don't think one of *us* did it, do you?" I ask. "Why would we have reported it– and put the body in our own Inn?"

"Just covering all bases," he repeats, and taps his pen on the desk.

Honestly, that is very annoying. Also, I'm pretty sure it's to the tune of "It's a Small World" which I now have stuck in my head.

He nods his head and keeps studying the list. How many times can he read the same names over and over again?

The file folder that he brought in with him is stuffed with papers, and I can see the edge of a photo sticking out. It must be of Samantha's dead body on the bed because I can see her hand, the red nail polish, the white sheets.

"Don't you ever leave town?" he asks, looking up from the paper.

"Of course I do," I say a tad defensively. "I've just been really busy lately. I have to focus on the Inn."

He nods. "Your boyfriend works in New York, right?" he asks.

"Yes, at the Bank of America," I say.

"He's not on the list," he points out. "And he hasn't signed out on the guest book. I see you have a 'daily commuter' section."

"Oh er– he used to. Greg spends the week in New York, and then Summerside on the weekends. He... umm... doesn't think it's necessary to write it down every time he goes."

We actually nearly broke up because of that book. Greg thought I was being too possessive and trying to keep tabs on him. In the end I caved, but I have a little diary at home I keep of when he comes and goes. Honestly, it just seems wrong to have a less than perfect record just because one person doesn't want to be "monitored".

"His mother works in New York too, right?" he asks.

"Well, she's an interior designer so she usually works out of her home office. She lives in Summerside and just goes to New York for the day if she needs to."

Vivienne doesn't like my book either. She laughs and says she would never remember to do it every time so she told me to put her name in the "always coming and going" column. Except, that column doesn't exist, and it would make the book really cluttered if I tried to add it. I keep track of her in my diary, too.

"We haven't got any DNA from the room yet," he says, sitting back in his chair. "And from briefly talking to some people in town today, I can gather the victim wasn't liked very much."

"She did have a way of rubbing people the wrong way," I say. More like walking all over them and spitting on their happiness.

"You grew up with her, right?" he asks.

"Well, we were in the same classes, but I wasn't friends with her." I don't need to mention the fact that Samantha's whole purpose at school seemed to be dedicated to making my life a living hell. I feel my mother covered that pretty thoroughly last night.

"Who was friends with her?" he asks. "Maybe they were still in contact with her at the time of her death."

"Well, Tracy was her best friend," I say. "But I know they haven't spoken in years. And Tim, Tracy's husband. He was good friends with her, too."

"Did she have any boyfriends?" he asks.

"Just one," I say, and I can feel my face go red. "She dated Greg all throughout high school."

He studies me with his eyebrows raised.

"You haven't told him anything, have you?"

"No," I say, "but I can see where you are going with this, and you're wrong."

He nods his head and writes something down.

"So, what are you going to do next?" I ask.

"Wait for the forensics to come back. Keep trying to contact her mother. Ask around town some more. I'm going to New York tomorrow to speak with her boss and look around her apartment."

It would be interesting to see what Samantha's place looked like. I imagine it would be super modern, with sharp corners everywhere.

"Would you like to come?" he asks, and I open my eyes wider. I wonder if he can read my mind.

"Would that be *allowed*?" I ask. "Aren't only police supposed to be a part of the investigation?"

"Normally yes, but sometimes we bring civilians in when we think their expertise might help the case."

"I'm not an expert on anything though," I argue.

"Don't take this the wrong way, but you're a little… obsessive."

What? How am I *not* supposed to take that wrong?

And it is so untrue. I am not–

Alright, maybe just a little.

"So far we have next to no leads and no evidence. We have limited time left before we eventually get in contact with her mother, at which point this probably won't be kept quiet any longer. You knew her and you might be able to pick something up that I would overlook."

"Alright. I'm not sure I'm going to be able to help, but I'll try," I promise.

"Thanks," he says. "I'll pick you up at eight in the morning?"

"You know, maybe we should take my car," I say. "Your SUV kind of screams police car, my car is a little less flashy."

And honestly I cannot handle the drive to New York in that mess.

He studies me for a moment before shrugging.

The door opens to the staff room and my mother's head pops through the doorway. "Luisa said you kids might be in here."

"I was actually just leaving," Ben says, standing up.

"Detective Gable and I have to go to New York tomorrow. Do you think you can be at the Inn all day?" And not burn down the place, I choose not to add.

"Of course, you two have a nice time and don't worry about anything here."

I'm sure going through a dead woman's apartment is going to be the time of our lives.

Ben walks to the door and turns to me. "I'll be at your place for eight."

I nod.

As Ben walks through the doorway he stops and turns to my mom. "You were in New York last weekend, right Tara?"

"Yes," she says smiling at him. "I had a course I was taking."

My body tenses as he nods.

"See you tomorrow," he says before disappearing through the doorway.

I'm starting to regret I ever agreed to this.

Thank God I didn't tell him about the insurance money.

Eight

See, this is how a car ride should be. My jacket is neatly folded on the back seat, the car window is slightly rolled down, and the radio is set to the news, volume level five.

True to his word, Ben is at my house at exactly eight o'clock and sits quietly in the passenger seat while I do my five point checklist before the journey. Luckily he doesn't try and bring his coffee mug in the car, but if he had I stocked up the glove compartment with Lysol wipes- just in case.

We start off the journey in silence, the only movement from Ben is when he leans over and looks at my odometer with his eyebrows raised.

Honestly, there is nothing wrong with the slow lane. And there is also nothing wrong with going five miles under the posted speed limit. You never know if you are going to drive over black ice, or a deer may run out in the road.

I'll admit it is *unlikely* in October while driving on a city highway in the middle of the day. But not impossible.

"Can I ask you a question?" I ask as a truck flies

by us, blaring his horn.

"Sure," he answers.

"Why did you agree not to tell the media about the murder?" I ask.

He studies me for a minute and I can't tell what he's thinking.

"I know we contaminated the crime scene and there probably isn't much evidence. It's a pretty big risk you're taking; I'm sure it would be easier for you if you could openly interrogate people," I point out.

"Not necessarily. People get their backs up when they hear you're investigating a murder. Even if they are completely innocent, they tend not to tell you too much because they think we are going to somehow magically blame them for everything," he replies. "Besides, we don't release any information to the public before we are able to contact the next of kin."

"Okay," I say, nodding.

"But if I'm being completely honest, that's not the real reason, that's just what I told the captain."

"So what is the real reason?" I ask.

He looks down at his hands before lifting his gaze to look out the window. "What you did with that Inn— it's amazing," he says. "My dad used to take me by it sometimes... he loved that old mansion. He used to like to do woodwork as a hobby and talked about all the architecture and molding inside it. He would have loved to see it restored, and he wouldn't have wanted me to destroy that."

For a moment I am lost for words.

"Thank you," I say.

"Okay, now my turn," he says, turning in his seat slightly.

I raise an eyebrow in his direction.

"What would you have done if I had said no to the whole firemen costumes deal?" he asks.

"I don't know," I shake my head. "My whole life is the Inn. The people in town would have understood eventually, but the guests... they either would be non-existent, or people that get off on murders and ghost stories. Not exactly the clientele I'm going for."

"What clientele is that?"

"I've always just wanted people to come stay at the Inn and feel included, like they are part of our family– our town," I say. "My dad used to take me to Inn when I was little, too. It was already abandoned at that point, but sometimes he would sneak me inside and let me slide down the banister."

"You slid down a banister?" he asks.

"I used to," I say.

"So you were a little adventurist as a child, and

then a bookworm as a teenager?" he asks.

I nod my head.

"When did you start dating Greg?" he asks.

"Greg moved to the city for college and I stayed here. He came back to visit Vivienne after he was done for Thanksgiving and we kind of hit it off," I shrug.

Hit it off would probably be the right way to describe it. Greg ran into the back of my car because he was on his cell phone and asked me to dinner to make it up to me. We had dinner the next day, and slowly over the next few months we just started seeing more and more of each other on the weekends. I just couldn't believe that someone like him– one of the *popular* kids– would be interested in me.

He was so attentive to me back then, always bringing me little gifts or saying the right things. Not that he's not now. I mean, I know he's just busy. He'll make it up to me when he gets a moment.

"Wasn't it ever weird for you? That he dated the woman who bullied you for most of your life?" he asks.

"I make it a point to not hold other people's mistakes against others; Greg's not like that. He didn't bully me, Samantha did," I point out. "Greg is great–"

I swallow the last word. Okay, maybe I do say it a little too much.

He sits quietly for a moment, mulling over my words. "Yeah, but he never did anything to stop it, either."

My movements become slow as I think about what he just said.

Well, it wasn't Greg's job to stand up for me. I can stand up for myself.

"What are you going to do when people actually find out that Samantha Manning was murdered at your Inn? Because, it will come out eventually. As soon as we tell Samantha's mother we have very little control over what is shared with the public."

I face forward with a determined look on my face, and try not to panic at what he is saying.

"I don't know. I'm just hoping that we can somehow find the killer before then, and explain it to the public in a way that won't hurt the Inn," I say.

"You know these things usually take a long time to solve. Unless there is evidence or a confession, it could take weeks, months, or even years," he says.

I turn my head and look in his eyes.

"Well, we better hurry up then," I put my foot down on the accelerator.

"Hello, Mr. Sanders. Thank you for meeting

with us on such short notice," Ben shakes his hand. "This is my assistant–"

"Candice Bourgoe," I say, interrupting Ben, and shake the man's hand. "It's French."

Ben raises his eyebrow to me and I return it with a smile. I came up with a whole fake identity for myself last night. I even managed to sketch out a brief family tree. You just never know who we might be talking to, what if Mr. Sanders was the one that killed Samantha? Do I really want a murderer knowing my real name?

"How can I help you?" he asks, sitting back in his chair.

Samantha works– er, worked– for Review, a website originating from New York City which specializes in reviewing the hospitality industry. Mr. Sanders' walls are lined with sleek silver photo frames, all depicting five star restaurants and hotels from all over the world that his company has reviewed.

The Inn could have been on this wall.

"Miss. Bourgoe," I notice Ben pauses on my name, and I send Mr. Sanders another smile, "and I are from the New York Times. We are planning on writing an article on some local, high profile critics, and one of your employee's name is being considered. Samantha Manning."

Mr. Sanders nods his head and sits forward in his chair, rubbing his chin. "Well, this is going to be a bit awkward, but Samantha Manning no longer works for this company."

"*What?*" I yell, and at Ben's look I clear my throat. "What I mean is, when did Miss. Manning leave the company?"

"We fired her a week ago," he says and shuffles the tidy papers in front of him.

What is going on here? If Samantha was fired, why did she come to the Inn to write a review?

"Can I ask why?" I say.

"We had a difference of opinion on many things," he says, averting his eyes. "I had to let her go."

"Difference of opinions on *what* exactly?" Ben asks.

"It was just a matter of personalities that clashed," he shrugs.

"I'm afraid you're going to need to be more specific than that, Mr. Sanders," Ben says.

"I'm afraid that's all I am able to say about the matter," he says, leaning back in his chair.

I see Ben's jaw tighten, obviously not pleased with the information a civilian can obtain, and I try to think quickly.

"Mr. Sanders, we appreciate that this is a delicate

matter. Because we are from similar industries I can appreciate the different personalities involved in the critiquing business. But we came here to write a story. Now, we can either ask around, perhaps talk to some of your clients, or some of your competitors, maybe even get Samantha Manning's side of the story. Or, we can extend you the professional courtesy of your company only being noted as one of her previous employers and hear your version of the story."

At his continued silence, I smile and pick up my bag. "There's one 'A' in Sanders, right? I just want to make sure I get it write for the headline."

"Alright, alright," he says and leans forward. "I'll tell you, but if I do, I have your word that we are kept out of the article, right?"

Ben leans forward as I nod.

"Samantha is a bitch, if you want me to put it bluntly. She goes around pissing the wrong people off all the time, and doesn't appreciate that those same people she is trampling all over are the ones that are funding our business."

"What do you mean, funding the business?"

"We like to call them 'gifts from appreciative clients'."

"You mean cut backs for five star reviews?" I ask.

"Don't look so surprised, everyone does it," he says.

I wonder how much my scented hands soaps and chocolates would have got me.

"Samantha had just wrote a scathing review for one of our clients who was willing to fund our project for the entire year, but she wouldn't listen to reason," he says, shaking his head. "I told her she was fired, and if I saw she had it printed somewhere else I would sue her for breach of contract."

"Who was the client?" Ben asks.

"No," he says shaking his head. "No names."

"What do you mean by breach of contract?" I ask.

"All my reviewers sign a contract when they start working here: any review written during their employment is owned by the company, and it is at our discretion whether we choose to print it or not."

"So, you print the reviews from people who give you money, and those who can't afford it get... what?" I say, rising from my seat. "Basically it's a 'pay up or you're out of business' venture you're running here?"

Ben rises and puts a hand on my arm.

"Oh, don't act so innocent. We all do it, it's called *sponsorship*," he says. "We print a wide range of reviews. There are some that do not get the best ratings, but that is not reflected by their lack of sponsorship. There are times when we write very good reviews for people that do not offer us any compensation."

"Yes, but with a sponsorship the reader is made aware it is a paid advertisement," I argue. "What you are doing is helping the rich get richer!"

"We had a deal," he says, pointing his finger at me. "None of this goes in your article."

"Don't worry," I spit out. "Your name is already in print more than it deserves to be."

"Well, that was interesting," Ben says as we get back in the car and drive to Samantha's apartment. "I would have liked to see her old office, but it probably wasn't the right time to ask by the end."

"Sorry," I say, gripping the steering wheel. "But, do you know how hard I worked to make sure everything was perfect for that review? I had a bikini wax for that woman!"

Well, half of one.

Ben raises his eyebrows, but thankfully says nothing.

"And you want to know what the worst part is? I actually kind of *admire* her for getting fired. At least she was standing up for what she believed in," I say.

"Kate, don't kid yourself. Samantha sounds like

she was a real piece of work. My hunch is she wrote that article just to piss people off."

"So, what now?" I ask.

"We go to her place and see if we can get any information on who the client was," he says.

"You think that's who could have killed her?" I ask.

"Who knows? But it's the only decent lead we've got."

"How are we going to get in?"

"I have her key," he says, fishing through his pocket and bringing out a pile of old receipts and wrappers. He finds the key with some pocket lint attached to it and holds it up for me to see.

"Is that legal, to go into her place without a warrant?" I ask, parking the car in front of Samantha's building.

"I have a warrant," he says, opening his door and getting out. "But, you are not on it, so if anyone asks, you work for the police department."

I run after him into the building's lobby, looking around to see if anyone is going to shout out that I don't belong there. I catch up to him at the elevator as he waits for the doors to open.

"Could I get arrested for this?" I whisper and frantically look around again.

"By who? I'm the police," he gets in the

elevator.

I quickly scramble in as well and watch as he presses the button for her floor.

"So, what are we looking for when we get inside?" I ask and take out my little clipboard from my purse.

"Whatever looks odd," he says, looking at my clipboard and frowning.

"Okay."

Look for odd things, I write.

"What are you doing?" he asks.

"Making a list."

"A list of what?"

"Of things to look for," I say. Honestly.

"Does that actually help you?" he asks. "All those checklists and rules?"

"Of course," I say and can't help but frown. "This way I can make sure everything is done properly and we won't waste any time."

He looks thoughtful before asking, "What happened to the girl who slid down the banister?"

My hand suddenly stops writing and I put my clipboard back in my purse.

"She doesn't exist anymore," I say.

When the doors finally open at Samantha's floor I am the first to get off.

Samantha's apartment is just as I imagined it, all

sleek lines and chrome accents; it must have cost her a fortune. It looks so cold– just like her. There are pictures of her everywhere, showing places she visited all over the world. And there isn't a picture of anyone else in sight.

"She sure has a lot of mirrors," Ben says, standing beside me in her living room, trying to take it all in.

"She had to look perfect all the time," I say, and look around the room feeling sorry for her yet again. Maybe that was why she was so cold. From this apartment, it seems as though she didn't have anyone who cared about her.

"Okay, we can't stay long, and we can't disturb anything in case we need to bring a team in to look for forensics. I'll look in here and the kitchen and you look in the bedroom. I have no idea what we are looking for, so just try and go with your gut," he says, and after I take a step I feel his hand on my arm, stopping me. "And, don't touch anything."

"Okay," I say, nodding, and he lets my arm go. I make my way to her bedroom and hesitate before finally walking in. A person's bedroom seems so private to me; it says more about the person than any other room in the home.

She was meticulously tidy and I gasp when I look in her closet. It is like my own personal heaven.

Every shelf is labeled, with her clothes sorted first by color, then by length. She even has a shelf for her nail polishes, lined up from a light beige to a medium pink.

I quickly take out my cell phone and take a picture. My closet at home is okay, but this is something else. Maybe when this is all over I will knock down the wall into the spare bedroom and do mine just like this. I could even have a special shelf for my clipboards!

Wandering around the bedroom nothing seems out of place to me. I idly wander into the connecting bathroom but the countertops are pretty bare, probably because she took most of her toiletries with her to the Inn.

One of the drawers is slightly ajar, and I look over my shoulder to make sure Ben can't see before I take out my pen from my purse and inch it open. I'm not *technically* touching anything. My pen is.

My eyes go wide as I see what is sitting on the top of the drawer.

Samantha took a *pregnancy test?*

I step back as what this means sinks in. That must be it! That must be who killed her. Maybe she went to the father, told him about the pregnancy, and he couldn't handle it. I shake my head, trying to comprehend how anyone could kill someone because they don't want to be a father.

But, what if he was married to someone else?

I open my mouth to call for Ben, but stop when I see something poking out from underneath the pregnancy test box.

I take the tip of my pen and gently nudge the box to the side.

Oh my God.

Forgetting all about disturbing any evidence I pick it up and quickly close the drawer as I hear Ben's footsteps approaching. I shove it down deep inside my coat pocket and turn just as he enters the bathroom.

"Got anything?" he asks.

"Nope," I say, trying to make my face neutral.

"Me neither," he says and studies me from under his lashes. "You okay?"

"Fine. It's just a bit... umm... unnerving being here. In her home," I say. "Can we go home now?"

"Sure," he says, still studying me.

I give him a quick smile before squeezing past him in the doorway and walking to the front door.

"Maybe I should drive home?" Ben asks and I don't even attempt to argue with him. To be honest I'm not sure if I could drive at this point.

I hand him my keys and get into the passenger

side, putting on my seat belt.

He keeps shooting me glances the whole way home but thankfully doesn't say much. We make most of the journey in silence which I am very grateful for. I have a lot to think about, starting with why Greg's business card was in Samantha's bathroom drawer.

Nine

I am a criminal. There is no use in trying to sugar coat it. I stole evidence from a crime scene (which is currently in my underwear drawer because I couldn't think of one other place I know no one will look), which basically makes me a wanted fugitive.

I have no idea why I took it to begin with. It was a knee jerk reaction, and a part of me really wants to go and steal that key from Ben's pocket so I can just put the card back in Samantha's bathroom and let someone else figure it out. But how could I do that to Greg? I don't even know what the card means.

It probably means nothing, in which case, I really did do the right thing. Ben already has it out for Greg, and if he saw that card he wouldn't leave it alone. He wouldn't forget about it. It would consume his attention. Trust me, I know.

"Come on, Maggie," I say, trying to pull her away from a fire hydrant she has been inspecting for the last fifteen minutes. "Mommy has to get back to work."

The dog stubbornly refuses to move. I thought

I read somewhere that dogs are used in therapy to help relieve people's anxiety and stress.

Honestly, I think this dog might be my undoing.

"Come on!" I say and lean my whole weight against the leash, trying to pull Maggie away from the hydrant.

Great, not only do I have barely any breasts or a butt, but a poodle weighs more than me. There is just no justice.

"You know, I once had a bitch like that," Mr. Phelps says from behind me. I slowly stand up straight again as I take in the little man standing behind me. I don't think I have ever seen Mr. Phelps not hunched over, even when I was a little girl he always seemed old to me. He has to be at least ninety, yet he walks around the town, all day long. I have absolutely no idea what he's doing, and I have a suspicion neither does he.

"She's not listening because you're too wishy washy with her," he says, scolding me.

"I am not–" I say, offended, but then see Maggie start to chew on the leash. "What do you mean?"

"You ask her to do things, even when you tell her to do them. Your voice is too high pitched," he says.

I put my hand to my throat.

"You need to show her the consequences when

she doesn't listen to you, because she isn't taking you seriously."

I look sharply at Maggie, flabbergasted. Honestly, she doesn't think I can be in charge? I'm always in charge.

"You have to really mean it," he says before walking away.

Once he has gotten out of ear shot I turn back to Maggie.

"Alright, listen Maggie. I am the boss," I say in the deepest voice I can manage. "Now, come here!"

I point to the floor beside me and pull on the leash. Suddenly another dog walks by and Maggie jumps up and starts walking beside him.

Well, it's not exactly what I was aiming for, but at least it's the right direction.

I stop at the post office to drop off a parcel for one of the guests. I reach down to untie Maggie from the lamppost, but stop when I see Ben walk across the street towards me. Quickly, I grab the leash and jump behind the hedge out of sight.

Maggie obediently comes along and sits down beside me.

"Oh, so now you listen," I say as we stare at each other.

I peek my head over the top of the hedge and freeze when I see who he crossed the road to talk to.

Vivienne just came out of the pharmacy and smiles at Ben when he approaches her.

What is Ben talking to Vivienne for? Is it something to do with Greg? Does he know about the card?

No, that's crazy. I am just being paranoid.

I lift my head slightly over the hedge so I can get a better angle as I desperately strain my ears to hear what they are saying. I can't hear anything, but my eyes are fixed to their lips. You know, it's been on my list for years to learn how to lip read, but unfortunately for me– in this particular moment– I just haven't been able to make room on my "Weekend Fun Projects List". Somehow it always gets trumped by relabeling the spice rack or alphabetizing my new books.

"Kate?" my mother asks from behind me, and I quickly turn around and pull her arm so she is behind the hedge too.

"Hi Mom," I say, trying to nonchalantly lean on the hedge.

"What are you doing?" she says, looking from Maggie to me.

"Nothing?" I shrug. "Maggie and me just decided to go for a walk."

"No, I mean what are you doing behind the hedge?" she asks.

"Just taking a break from the sun," I fan myself dramatically.

My mom peers over the hedge and smirks. "Yes, I suppose things have been a little hotter than usual in town."

"I don't know what you mean," I say and cautiously look back over the hedge.

"You know I've seen the way he looks at you, too," my mother says.

"Mother! No he doesn't," I say, shaking my head. "Ben is just being nice to me because he wants my help with the case. It's his *job.*"

"Okay," she says with a placating smile. "And you spend all your time thinking about him because…"

"Because I want this case to be solved so everything can go back to normal," I say. "And I don't spend all my time thinking about him!"

"Okay," she repeats.

Honestly, I don't. I've only had to think about him recently because of the case. If it weren't for that he wouldn't cross my mind.

Seriously.

"You've always been the worst judge of character," my mother says to me while she pats Maggie on the head.

"What is that supposed to mean?" I say, but then

lower my voice as I think I see Vivienne's head turn in my direction.

"You give people chances over and over again when they don't deserve it, and then when someone finally comes along that is worth it, you push them away," she says, and I can't tell anymore if she is talking about Ben or herself.

"I don't push people away," I argue.

They usually just naturally run away.

My mother doesn't say anything else, but we continue to squat next to each other, peering over the hedge.

Ben is still talking to Vivienne, who is just enamored with him. She is constantly putting her hand on his arm, and throwing her head back in laughter.

Well, I don't have to be able to read lips to say I'm fairly certain he isn't accusing her son of killing Samantha.

"What do you think they're saying?" Mom asks, squinting her eyes.

I think this is the thing I love the most about my mother. She always gets fully invested in what she is doing, whether she knows what is going on or not. From the concentration on her face you would think we were solving some great mystery and she's a part of the thrilling adventure.

"I don't know. He could have either just said "you should go" or "so you know". It's a tough call."

"What are you two doing?" Tracy says from behind us, and my mother and I both jump.

Mom quickly puts her finger to her lips to tell Tracy to be quiet and waves her down next to us.

Tracy squats and peers over the hedge as well.

"What are we looking at?" she asks.

"Detective Gable," my mother answers.

"Oh good," Tracy says, smiling, and puts her bag on the ground.

"We are just trying to get out of the sun for a minute," I say to them both, though I am already looking back over the hedge again.

"Don't worry, I won't tell Greg," Tracy winks at me. "Because I can't say I blame you for staring. Though, if Tim ever asks, I was only doing it for moral support for you."

I roll my eyes.

"Have you seen him jog yet?" Tracy asks, and to my shock my mother smiles and nods.

"When does he jog?" I ask, frowning.

"About five in the morning," Tracy says, then produces some candy out of her purse and offers me some. "I stand by the window and watch with my morning coffee."

"Does he go East or West?" my mother asks,

reaching her hand into the bag.

"East usually," Tracy says.

"Honestly, don't you two have anything better to do?" I say, shaking my head.

"Like you're doing right now?" Tracy asks, and I have to begrudgingly turn away.

She might have a point. Though it's not what they think. I'm obviously not ogling Ben for eye candy. My observing him is strictly professional.

"Do you think he wears boxers or briefs?" Tracy asks, tilting her head to the side.

"Boxers," I say, nodding decisively. The blush spreads up my neck as I realize how quickly I answered.

"You know Kate, no one would blame you if you went for Ben," Tracy says, nonchalantly.

"Well, I'm sure Greg might. Considering he's my boyfriend," I say, and at their lack of belief in my statement I put my hands on my hips.

"He would!" I argue.

Tracy smiles and nods, "Of course he would. Greg obviously cares about you."

I stare at Tracy. Cares about me? Why do I get the impression that she chose that word carefully?

Not that it's a bad word. I mean, obviously it's nice for someone to care about you. But Greg does more than that; he *loves* me. And I love him.

At least, I'm pretty sure I kind of do.

I mean, we have been together for two years, you don't just abandon that because he might have impregnated another woman and killed her, do you?

Alright, well when you phrase it like that it doesn't seem so confusing.

But it is because Greg probably didn't do any of that. And here we are, all sitting behind a bush and staring with puppy dog eyes at a man because he can jog.

And he does have very nice shoulders.

But, that's not the point. The point is, we are all being disloyal to Greg here.

"What is happening?" Luisa's head appears between Tracy and me as she gets on her knees between us.

"We are watching Ben," my mother says.

"No we are not! We are simply observing a conversation between two people while trying to stay out of the sun," I tell them all.

"What are they talking about for so long?" Tracy asks. We all watch Vivienne's hands wave around dramatically while she tells Ben a story. He seems to be listening intently and nodding at the appropriate times. I really hope they aren't talking about me.

Not that they would. I mean, I am not one of those people that thinks the world revolves around them.

But honestly, besides me, what do they even have in common?

Of course, Vivienne is a very attractive woman. But she is old enough to be his mother, and Ben doesn't seem like he would be interested in Vivienne's type. You know, the dyed hair, painted nails, always looking like they walked out of a magazine. Who has time for that?

Not that it isn't a free country... I mean, he's welcome to do whatever he wants.

Except date Vivienne.

Oh God, I sound like my mother.

"Mr. Ben is so strong, he helped me move things around in the trastero yesterday," Luisa says, placing her head on the hedge with a moony look in her eyes. "I keep thinking how he can toss me around, too."

"Luisa!" I say, but my mother and Tracy just smile.

"He lost his mama as a baby. I show him the iron yesterday and he look like he never seen it before," she says. "I iron *whatever* he want."

Honestly, this whole thing is getting ridiculous.

"What's going on?" I hear from behind me and turn to see Becky staring at the four of us behind the hedge.

"Is no one at the Inn?" I wonder, looking

around.

"Mr. Patterson asked me to get light bulbs," Becky says, holding up the plastic bag in her hand.

"I have to go back to work," I declare and stand up, grabbing Maggie's leash.

"Oh okay," my mother says, nodding.

"Becky, can you take Maggie home on your way?" I ask.

"Sure, come on Maggie," she takes the leash and the dog springs up and starts to walk right beside Becky down the street.

Maybe I need to read that obedience book a third time.

"Aren't you three coming?" I ask.

"In a minute," Tracy waves away my question. "I just want to see if he runs back to his car."

I roll my eyes as my mother reaches into Tracy's bag again for another candy.

Ten

I just need to take a moment and think about this logically. If I can figure out a marriage proposal in seven minutes just based on my mother's facial expressions, I think I can figure out why Greg's business card was in Samantha's bathroom.

I just need to go over the facts.

1. Greg's business card was underneath a pregnancy test in Samantha's bathroom.
2. Samantha wrote a review and got fired because of it.
3. Samantha came here to write a review even though she didn't work for the company anymore.
4. Samantha is dead.

I stare at the list for ages, but I just can't seem to connect anything. It just doesn't make sense.

What was Greg's card *doing* there? Was he seeing her?

No, I can't believe that. I know things haven't been exactly great between us lately, but we're just in a rut. Every couple gets like that from time to time.

And plus, if my boyfriend was seeing someone

else, I think I would *know*. I know everything.

Alright, not everything. I never could get calculus. But *this* I would know.

And the worst part is, I can't even ask him about it. I would have to explain to him why I was in Samantha's house, and that just isn't an option. Not that I don't trust Greg, I just don't want him to say something in an offhand gesture, and have Ben hear. Greg can be a little obtuse sometimes, maybe because he is used to being in charge at his job. Sometimes he will flippantly say something I've specifically asked him not to mention, and he kind of just shrugs like it's no big deal. Like the time Vivienne wanted to redecorate my house for me and I told Greg I wanted to do it myself. I really like Vivienne, and I think she's talented, but her taste is just way too contemporary for me. I had a great plan: tell her I just didn't have the money for new things and I was going to try and find some good bargains online, but Greg just told her at dinner that night that I didn't want her to do it. Later, when I was fuming at him in the car ride home, he shrugged and said it was better just to say things the way it is so people don't get confused. But, he could tell I was still really mad, so he said he would make it up to me.

See, if Greg was seeing Samantha, wouldn't he just tell me?

Suddenly I know exactly what to do. I haven't talked to Greg since dinner the other night, which isn't that unusual because he's usually really busy with work during the week, so I speak to him mainly on the weekends. But, if I just call him and hear the sound of his voice, I know I will feel much better.

After a minute or so of ringing, I finally hear the click in my ear.

"Hello?" Greg's voice sounds distant, and I can hear a lot of people in the background competing with the music.

"Greg!" I say. "How are you?"

"Kate?" he asks, sounding unsure.

"Yes!" Oh thank God, he recognized my voice. See, of course he's not cheating on me.

"It's hard for me to hear you," he says, shouting loudly into the phone.

"Where are you?"

"Just having some drinks with a client," he replies.

I look down at my watch and lift my eyebrows. It's ten am, which is a bit early for a drink.

I don't know how those New Yorkers do it.

"Listen Kate, I'm kind of busy. Can I call you back later?" he asks, and I can hear the waiter ask if he wants a refill.

"Yes, of course. Not a problem," I say.

A little nagging feeling is still in the pit of my stomach, and I decide I won't rest assured if we end the conversation now.

"It's a shame about the review, huh?" I ask. "That Samantha couldn't stay."

I wait to hear even the slightest hint of a reaction from him. Any slight pause, but he answers nonchalantly, "Yeah. I'm sure you can get someone else to do it, though."

"Yeah, you're right."

No reaction, that's a good sign. Though, I can't help but feel I am perhaps not asking the right questions.

"It's just so weird she would leave like that. She seemed fine to you at the dinner the other night, right? She wasn't upset about anything?"

Like, perhaps, you being the father of her unborn child?

"Not that I remember," he says, and I relax at his offhanded tone. "Listen, Kate, I really have to go."

"Of course. I'll see you this weekend," I say. "Oh, Tracy and Tim left a bottle of wine for you at my house to say thanks for getting them those art gallery tickets the other week."

"Oh yeah, it's a shame we couldn't go. I know you were looking forward to it," he says.

There, I knew it. Greg isn't cheating on me. He loves me.

"You had a business dinner, right?" I ask.

"Yeah, with those clients from Goldman Sachs. They're not making my life easy at the moment," he says, sighing. "I'll see you on the weekend."

I hear the click in my ear and he's gone. I slowly lower the receiver and try to stop my hand from shaking.

Goldman Sachs? He told me is was Silverman's Mines.

Why would he *lie* about that? Did he just get confused? He sounded pretty busy, maybe he just mixed up the names.

I look at the business card that has been staring at me since I got back yesterday.

I can't tell Ben about Greg's card. I mean, I have no idea what it means, but I know Greg and he isn't capable of murdering anyone. If I tell Ben about the card I would just be opening a can of worms, and he would be distracted instead of trying to find the real murderer.

Greg is so successful; he gives his business card to everyone he meets. It's kind of embarrassing actually: he even brings them to the grocery store and hands them to the cashiers.

Samantha could have gotten his card anywhere; it's just bad luck that it was in her drawer under that test.

The trouble is, I don't quite believe it myself right now, so what chance do I have of Ben believing it?

Sighing, I look up from the reception desk and out the window to see that the storage shed's door is open and banging in the strong wind.

I just can't catch a break.

I reach behind me for my trench coat hanging on the coat rack. I push both my arms through the sleeves and shaking my head take the belt and tightly cinch it around my waist. As I double knot the ties I realize I've tied it too tight in my frustration and confusion, but the constant banging makes me decide to ignore the constricting feeling around my center. Leaving through the side entrance, I make my way quickly over the hundred yards to the storage shed with my head down, trying to block some of the wind from sending chills all over my body.

When I reach the shed I realize that the door hasn't swung open by itself. The banging from inside lets me know someone is in there, but I just saw Mr. Patterson out front trimming the hedges, so it can't be him. Thinking one of the guests has taken it upon themselves to get a tool of some sort I shake my head and tell myself not to scream at them to get out.

"Excuse me, there are no guests allowed in here," I say to the back of the large black windbreaker that is hunched over the workbench.

"One second, I'm just looking for some sandpaper," they respond in a muffled voice.

"Ben?" I yell over the wind and suddenly feel my body tense. "What are you doing in here?"

"I've already told you," he says, turning around to quickly take in my position before returning to his task. "You don't happen to know where a hammer is, do you? It's not very organized in here."

"I wouldn't know; I'm not responsible for the storage shed. Mr. Patterson is. I'm sure he has his own system." I say, feeling like I have to defend the untidy space, though I have no idea why. I have talked to Mr. Patterson so many times about organizing this shed, but he always absently nods like he's not listening to me. I feel we have come to a mutual understanding that as long as the door is closed, he will pretend he is working on it, and I will try not to obsess over it every time I look outside. It's worked pretty well so far.

"I'm glad you're here anyways," Ben says, but doesn't turn around. "I've been thinking a lot about the other day in New York."

My body goes completely still and I swallow the lump in my throat. I knew he knew something was wrong. He's never that quiet, and he didn't even drive in the fast lane on the way home.

"Oh?" I manage to eventually get out.

"Something is bothering me about Samantha's place, and I wanted to get your opinion on it," he says.

I nod even though he can't see me.

He turns with the sandpaper and hammer in his hand.

"I think Samantha might have been seeing someone," he says.

"Really?" I reply, my voice slightly breaking. "I– what makes you think that?"

"There was a pair of men's leather shoes in the front closet,"

Okay don't freak out. Breathe, just breathe.

The closeness of Ben's body and the confined space make me suddenly feel very claustrophobic. And the uncomfortably tight belt around my waist isn't helping either. My fingers quickly start working on undoing the knot, but it won't give an inch. "Well, those could be anyone's. Maybe she had a friend over, and he forgot them."

Ben leans in closer so our bodies are only a foot apart. "He left without his shoes on?"

"Maybe it was raining, and he didn't want to ruin the leather," I offer as my fingernails dig into the knot, urging it to separate, my chest starting to ache. "Or maybe they are her brother's."

Ben's jaw tightens before he shakes his head.

"You and I both know she didn't have any brothers."

I hold my hand up to say something, but I have to gasp for breath. "Or maybe–" I stop speaking and grip Ben's arm for support, trying to take deep breaths.

"Kate?" The worried tone of Ben's voice is mirrored by his features as he puts his hand under my chin to study my face. "What's wrong?"

"My belt–" I say between gasps. "I tied it... too tight... can't get air..." I know I'm starting to hyperventilate, but I can't control my breathing.

Ben quickly transfers the hammer and sandpaper into my hands, his fingers reaching for the belt that is secured around my waist. His larger hands have even more trouble with the small knot than mine did. He quickly turns around to survey the workbench, his eyes searching as it becomes increasingly hard for me to stand. I start to lose focus, and the hazy feeling lets me know that loss of consciousness is fast encroaching. The sound of Ben banging and throwing things is the only noise that I can hear as the weight of my eyelids is becoming more than I can handle.

The banging suddenly stops and I hear Ben come back to where I'm standing. I see a glint of something silver before his hand is on the belt, and suddenly I feel an immense sense of release. I sink to the ground, with Ben's arms guiding me. I hear my own breath coming in desperate, wheezing gasps.

"Kate, where is your inhaler?" he asks, and I feel him reaching in my pockets to search for it.

Tears stream down my face and I can't get any air into my lungs. I try and grab his arm in a pleading gesture, but he shakes it off and I hear the shed door bang open again and he's gone.

It seems like minutes, but it could only have seconds before I hear Ben's rushed steps return. My body is shaking from the lack of oxygen.

Ben grabs my face and I feel the cold object shoved in my mouth, a gust of cold medicine forcing my lungs to expand.

He gathers me in his arms, stroking my hair. "Breathe, just breathe," he says, his warm embrace so comforting.

My breath turns from wheezing gasps, to short breaths. Slowly, I'm able to take deep breathes and my arms wrap around Ben's waist.

"Are you okay?" he asks.

"I usually have it in my pocket," I say. I don't know what to say, but that is the first thing that comes out of my mouth.

"I'm going to call an ambulance," he says, and tries to remove my arms from around his waist.

"No, I'm okay. I'll be okay," I assure him and

wrap my arms more tightly around his waist so he won't get up.

"You shouldn't be having this many attacks," he says, but thankfully doesn't try to move. "We need to get you to a doctor."

"I can keep it under control normally," I say. "This past week is the first time I have had to use my emergency inhaler in years."

"Were you born with it?" he asks.

I shake my head. "I developed it after my father left."

"Why did he leave, Kate?" he asks, and when he feels my body tense he adds, "Forget it, you don't have to answer that."

"My father had obsessive compulsive disorder," I say in a soft tone. "He left because he couldn't cope with us anymore."

Ben doesn't say anything, but I feel his arms tighten around my back.

"You've met my mother, so there is no big mystery there as to why. If she can find her keys she counts it as a good day."

"Well, I'm sure he knew that when they got married," Ben points out.

I can't help but smile at the way my mother has already charmed Ben around her little finger.

"I don't blame her for his leaving. I was angry

when I was younger and took it out on her, but I never blamed her," I say. "We tried to find him, but he disappeared. We got a letter from his girlfriend a few years ago to say he had passed away of a stroke."

"I'm sorry," Ben says.

I just nod. There's nothing really else to say about it.

"Are you okay now?" he asks.

"Yes, I– what was the shiny thing you had in your hand before?" I ask, looking down.

"I had to cut your belt with a utility knife," he says, lifting the cut end.

"Oh," I say, still slightly confused from the lack of oxygen. "I'm not sure if I have another belt that matches this coat."

The soft chuckle from Ben brings my gaze from the belt to his face.

"What?"

"I've never known a woman who would rather pass out than live with the possibility that her wardrobe might not be completely coordinated."

"I never said–" I say, but his voice interrupts my slow thoughts.

"I know, I was joking." He tucks my hair behind my ear, leaving his hand on the side of my cheek before untangling me from his arms and helping me to my feet.

We both stand in the storage shed, studying each other, wondering if the other one has given something away somehow. Taking a deep refreshing breath, I remember the weight in my hands and look down to see I am still tightly grasping the hammer and sandpaper.

"What are you doing with these, anyways?" I ask, giving them back to him.

"Trying to get into a lady's good graces," he says, taking them from me and putting his hand on my waist to guide me back to the Inn.

"What do you mean?" I ask.

"Mr. Patterson didn't get a chance to fix the banister yet, and his arthritis is really bothering him right now. My dad taught me how to fix things, so I volunteered to help him."

"You know, it's against the Inn's rules to allow guests to use the tools for liability reasons."

Ben opens the front door and helps guide me through. "Don't worry, I won't sue."

"You say that now," I argue and carefully sit down in the chair behind the reception desk, my legs still shaky.

"Kate, you can trust me," he says, and I look at the serious look in his eyes.

"I know," I say.

"Whatever the problem is, I'll help you," he says,

and my eyes can't look away from the intensity of his stare. "I wouldn't let anything hurt you, or the Inn."

I'm not sure if it's because of what happened in the shed, or because he has stuck his neck out for me more this week than anyone has ever done for me, but my eyes smart with tears.

"Thank you," I say.

He waits for me to say something more, but the door opens and my mother comes flying in.

"Hey kids," she says, ruffling Ben's already messy hair before coming over and kissing me on the cheek. "Did I miss lunch?"

"No, we are just about to serve it," I say and quickly shoot my gaze in Ben's direction.

"I'll work on the banister while everyone's in the dining room and have my lunch later," he says.

"Oh, I was hoping you would be able to join us," my mother pouts her bottom lip. "Can't it wait?"

"I better not; I've got to go over some things with my team on the case this afternoon. There's been some new developments," he says but doesn't look at me, instead keeping his eyes on my mother's face.

"Okay, I'll make sure Luisa brings you a sandwich," my mother says, taking off her coat and smiling.

"Thanks," he looks at me only for a second before walking down the hallway to the staircase.

"Developments are good," my mother says in a hopeful tone. "Maybe this whole thing will be over with soon. Though, I'll be so sad to see Ben go. I've become rather fond of him."

I force a smile and nod before returning my attention back to the reservation book.

The problem is, so have I.

Eleven

Ben left right after lunch yesterday, and I haven't seen him since. To make matters worse, the storm has knocked out our phone lines, and the town's cellphone tower is also not operating at the moment. Everyone is feeling a little antsy not being able to get in contact with anyone, but I have tried to assure them we are working on getting it fixed.

Mom organized a game of charades in the lounge earlier this evening and it seemed to lighten everyone up a little. I even had a turn, and my team was very close to winning a round.

I had Becky and Luisa on my team, and it turns out neither of them have heard of the Sound of Music *(I know, right?)*. I did an excellent silent remake of the entire movie, though. "I Am Sixteen, Going On Seventeen" was the highlight, by far.

Mom and I are sitting in the dining room, which is full tonight with all our guests. We decided to ask everyone to dress informal to keep the fun mood going, and we've pushed all the tables together to form a big circle to serve the dinner family style. I'm laughing at a funny story told by Mr. Shaw when the dining room door flings open.

My mother nearly jumps out of her seat from the bang and I put my hand on her arm in a reassuring gesture.

There, in the doorway, is Samantha's mother. She stands slightly hunched over, and I can tell from her uneven breathing that she has been drinking.

"You," she says, pointing at me. "You did this!"

My eyes widen, and I stand up.

"Mrs. Manning, I haven't done anything. If we could just go to the lounge– " I start, but she interrupts me.

"Not you," she says, waving her arm like she is trying to swat away a fly. "You!"

I follow her gaze to my mother, who sits with a steely look on her face.

"Stephanie, I haven't done anything, and you're drunk."

"Like hell you didn't," she spits out the accusation. "You murdered my baby!"

The guests, in unison, let out a shocked gasp.

"Mrs. Manning, let's go to the lounge where we can talk about–" I try and approach her, but she shoves me into the wall.

I see Ben enter from the kitchen doorway. He takes one look at me and then moves his gaze to Samantha's mother. "What the hell is going on?" he asks.

My mother is on her feet now, and comes to stand between me and Mrs. Manning. "I haven't killed anyone Stephanie, but if you lay one more finger on my daughter I might be tempted."

Mrs. Manning's face passes from worry to amusement in a flash. "That threat is getting a bit old now, don't you think?" she asks.

"Maybe it's time I actually followed through," my mother suggests.

I frown as I look between the two women.

"You were jealous when you couldn't keep your husband away from me then, and you're just jealous my daughter is more successful than yours now."

I put my hand to my mouth at Mrs. Manning's implication and look to my mother for her reaction.

"I don't like to speak ill of the dead, Stephanie. Because you just lost your daughter, I am going to pretend you never said that."

"*Lost my daughter?*" she yells. "She was murdered! At your Inn!"

"And Detective Gable is doing everything he can to make sure the murderer is found and arrested," my mother says, never taking her eyes from Mrs. Manning's face.

"What was she even doing here?" she asks, looking around wildly as though the answer is written on the wall somewhere.

"She came to write a review, like you asked her to," I remind her.

"I didn't ask her anything!" she says, looking at me again. "I told your mother that I had done her all the favors she deserved in this life– keeping your father entertained all those years ago."

She laughs hysterically and sends herself off balance again.

Ben comes to stand beside her, grabbing her arm. "Mrs. Manning, you've had terrible news today. I'm going to take you back to the police station."

She tries to pull her arm free. "I'm not going anywhere with you!" she yells.

"I wasn't asking," he says, putting his other hand on her shoulder to lead her out of the dining room.

I look around at the guests staring at me and I shake my head. "I'm so sorry, I–" I have no idea what to say to them. "Excuse me."

I walk out of the dining room and through the hallway to the reception area where I put my hands on the desk for support.

"Kate?" My mother says hesitantly from behind me.

"Is it true?" I ask, and when she doesn't reply I turn to face her. "Did he have an affair with Mrs. Manning?"

My mother pauses before running her hands through her hair. "Your father was a complicated man, Kate. He had a disorder."

"Did he have an affair with Mrs. Manning?" I ask, more forcefully this time.

"Yes," she answers. "When I found out I asked him to stop."

"Did he?" I ask, though I already know the answer.

"No," she sighs. "In the end I told him he needed to stop, or he couldn't see you anymore. I didn't want you to be the laughing stock of the town because your father couldn't control himself."

"So he left," I say, slowly lowering myself into the reception chair.

"I couldn't tell you before. I didn't want you to hate me—" Mom breaks off as tears roll down her face. "I knew he wouldn't stop for me, but I had convinced myself he would control himself for you; instead my pushing just forced him to leave."

This is just too much. Too much has happened. There is too much to process. I feel my mind shutting down, my body going detached and cold. I just can't do this right now. Any of it.

The front door opens as Ben comes back inside. "Detective Rice is taking Mrs. Manning back to the station," he says, looking from my mother to me.

"I'm sorry. I tried to call and warn you that we had finally got in contact with her but–"

"Our phone lines have been down all day," I explain, and am surprised at how remote and detached my voice sounds.

"I will speak to her, try and keep it out of the papers…" my mother offers, but I shake my head.

"There's no point. Our guests all know, the story will be all over town within the hour," I say, getting up and picking up my coat and purse.

"Kate, you can't leave here like this–" Ben says and grabs my arm to stop me.

I look him in the eye and offer a small smile. "I'm fine. I knew this was coming."

"Where are you going?" he asks.

"I just need to be alone right now," I say after he releases my arm.

"I'll come by your house later to make sure you're okay," he says, but I shake my head.

"I'll be fine. I just want to go to bed." I do feel sleepy. I am just so tired.

His jaw tightens and I can see the argument building behind his eyes, but my mother comes up and puts her hand on his shoulder. "I'll check on her later, Ben. You go and deal with Stephanie."

He looks from my mother, back to me, and eventually nods.

"I'll see you tomorrow," I say to no one in particular and open the door, heading for my car in the parking lot.

My whole life: it was all a lie. I built my father up to be this mystical being that was forever smiling in my head, ready to catch me at the end of the banister rail. When all this time he left because he couldn't keep out of other women's beds.

I thought it was her fault. I never blamed her, but deep down I always thought if my mother had just tried a bit harder, if we had kept the house a little neater, he would never have left.

I feel like everything I have ever known is just a figment of my imagination. I didn't really know him at all.

Which is why I need to go and find out if I have convinced myself of something else as well.

Greg isn't home when I get to his apartment in the city a few hours later. It's just as well; this whole thing will probably be easier if I don't have to figure out if he is lying through his shiny teeth or not. I'm going to look at the facts and let them speak for themselves.

I bring my clipboard inside— honestly right now I feel like it's the only stable thing in my life— and I am determined to write down anything that looks remotely suspicious. Then, I am going to go home, drink a whole bottle of wine (maybe two because, by God, I deserve it), and figure this whole thing out.

I use the spare key he gave me in case of emergency– this alone took me two years to get, and it's only because he slipped in the shower a few months ago and broke his arm, that he eventually caved.

His apartment is immaculate, which usually makes me gleeful, but when I look around all I see is a hollow shell of a home. There aren't any pictures of us anywhere, even though I printed one from our first date and put it in a nice frame for him for Christmas. He told me the frame didn't go with his décor so he was looking for another one.

It was black. What doesn't black go with?

I grab my pen from my purse

No pictures of me anywhere. Even though I have been told I am extremely photogenic and have a nice nose.

Standing here, looking around, I'm starting to remember other things about our relationship. I remember the time Greg took me white water rafting. I don't swim very well and I didn't really want to go, but it was one of our first dates and I couldn't say no. Also, I read a guide on white water rafting and watched multiple Youtube videos, so I thought I was prepared.

Well, I wasn't. The first time we got to one of the rapids our raft was bouncing all over the place and my helmet fell over my eyes. I took my hands off the sides of the boat to fix it just as we hit a huge rock, and I went flying out. I went down the rapids with just my life jacket and helmet, and was tossing all over the place, struggling to get my head above the water. I felt something tugging me down and kicked feverously until I heard Greg yelling.

"Jesus, Kate, stop kicking me!" I opened my eyes to see him in the raft, trying to hold onto my life jacket, and trying to keep me above water.

I was so relieved I started to cry. When I finally got back into the raft Greg frowned at me. "I thought you said you knew how to raft. Why did you let go?" he asked as though he was mad at me.

Like it was a choice I made to go down the rapids and get my legs and arms all scratched up when I don't even know how to swim properly.

"*What?*" I asked, my temper simmering in my eyes through my tears.

He must have seen me recoil from his angry tone because his scowl was quickly replaced with a smile. "It's okay," he said, putting his hand on my arm as though he decided to forgive me. "Maybe rafting wasn't such a good idea. Let me make it up to you, okay?"

He never did make it up to me, though. Come to think of it, he's never really made anything up to me.

I make my way into his bedroom. I'm not sure why exactly, but I started in Samantha's bedroom, so my gut is telling me that whatever I need to find will be in here.

I go to his nightstand and open the drawer, but the only thing inside is the latest bestseller from Tom Clancy, and his reading glasses sit on top. My hands desperately want to rip out the last page of his novel so he won't know how it ends, but I decide that's too spiteful. It would really drive him crazy, and plus I don't know if my suspicions are even true yet. Instead I pick up my pen.

Nothing hidden in his bedroom drawer.

Also, his glasses have a small scratch on the left lens.

You just never know what might be important.

Frowning I look at the other flat surfaces around the room, immaculately uncluttered, and shake my head. I'm not going to find anything here.

Sighing, I walk past the bed in hopes I might have better luck in the living room or bathroom when I see his closet door is open a crack. I pull the door the rest of the way and enter the walk-in closet, which is just as neat as the rest of the house. It's not as nice as Samantha's, but it is still nicer than mine.

He doesn't deserve a nicer closet than me.

I run my hands over his shirts and one accidently falls off the hanger onto a heap on the floor. I contemplate leaving it there, but know that Greg would probably suspect someone has been here if I do. He would never leave one of his shirts like that. I bend down to pick it up and I see a bright red photo box on a shelf below his pants.

Sitting on my heels, I put my clipboard down beside me and take the box off the shelf. Setting it on the floor in front on me, I shimmy the top off and toss the lid aside.

Sitting on top is a card with hearts and sparkles on the front.

"Remember on Valentine's Day you said we could do all my favorite things?"

I open the card and the message is *"My favorite thing is you."* Samantha's name is signed.

I move the card to the side, so I can see what else is inside. It is full of pictures of the two of them. Some are from when they were in high school, but I know some are only from a few weeks ago. I bought Greg the red sweater he's wearing in one where they are kissing and standing in front of a waterfall.

I guess she knew how to white water raft better than I do.

I lift the top few pictures and my eyes widen.

Apparently they also liked to take pictures of themselves when they weren't wearing any clothes at all.

I throw everything back in the box and shove it back on the shelf. I feel like I am outside of my body as I casually pick up my clipboard and make my way back to the front door. My body feels numb, and my mind has wandered off somewhere far, far away. A million thoughts should be going through my head right now; I should be making lists of everything this means.

Nothing. I feel... nothing.

As I reach for the handle to the front door I pause and open the door to the hall closet instead. Greg's shoes are neatly lined up in rows and there, in the middle of the fourth row, is a gap where the pair of shoes is missing.

It's silly. Seeing all of those pictures should have sent me over the deep end. But standing here, looking at the spot where the missing shoes should be– the shoes Ben found in Samantha's hallway closet– something inside of me finally snaps.

He would never keep anything at my house because he said he was afraid Maggie would chew it. I am going to find his most expensive pair and give them to Maggie for Christmas.

After picking out a fine pair of Italian loafers, I

quickly make my way back into his bedroom, open his night stand, and rip out the last page of his book.

The bastard will just have to suffer.

Twelve

You know what's a funny word? Tequila. At least, I'm finding it hilarious right now. I lost count after seven shots, but I think I've had a lot.

My clipboard is beside me in Joe's Tavern. I ordered it a martini a little while ago, because I'm not the only one who's had a trying week. My lists just haven't been the same lately, and I think my clipboard has noticed. I just got back from the dance floor, which I am proud to say I made myself out of a spare piece of plywood I found outside. Stanley, who is always in our town's one and only bar, is doing a pretty good rendition of Flashdance considering we just played vodka Ping-Pong for an hour.

I called Tracy an hour ago to come and have a drink with me, but so far she's only had coffee and keeps trying to convince me to let her take me home.

"Tracy, look at him go!" I yell over the music and begin to sing. *"I'm gonna live forever."*

I point my finger at Tracy and wait in anticipation.

"Fame."

"BABY REMEMBER MY NAME!" I slip off

my stool for the last note and am thrown into another giggling fit.

"Kate, do you think you're nearly ready to go home?" She puts her hand to her forehead. "I'm starting to get a pretty nasty headache."

"Oh, I think you just need another drink." I wave to the bartender, Mike, who looks at me and rolls his eyes.

"He'll be by in a minute," I assure her.

A bright light flashes over the bar, which means someone else has come through the door. The windows are pretty much blacked out from all the cigarette smoke over the years, and the owner thinks it's nostalgic not to clean them. Usually I look at those windows and wouldn't even consider coming inside. But, my decisions haven't exactly been the greatest ones lately, have they? So, I decided to give this place a try, and it is amazing! They have so much alcohol, and everyone is being really nice to me. Mr. Phelps even showed me how to take the peanut out of the shell without crumbling it everywhere.

And I will always be grateful to him for that.

Tracy turns around and I see relief written all over her face.

I turn around to see what she's looking at, though my eyes take a minute to focus. Ben stands behind us with his eyebrow raised, his hand on his hip.

"Detective Gable!" I say and unsteadily get off my chair.

"How many has she had?" he asks Tracy.

"At this point, who knows?" Tracy says, shrugging. "I got here about an hour ago, but she was already pretty gone."

"You called him?" I ask her, frowning. My eyes can't seem to find where she is standing. "You didn't have a nice time?"

"Honey, I have to get home. Tim is waiting for me. Ben's going to take you home, okay?"

I slowly drag my eyes from her face to his and turn around to get back on my stool.

"I'm not going home," I say and try and get Mike's attention again.

I feel Tracy kiss me on the cheek. "I'll call you in the morning."

I nod and throw one of the peanut shells in Mike's direction to get his attention. It falls a foot in front of me and I frown. Must have been a bad nut.

"Hey Mike, can I get a beer?" Ben asks, taking a seat on the stool beside me.

"Sure thing, Ben," he nods and picks up an empty glass.

"I want teqweela!" I yell at him.

"I've already told you that if you can't

pronounce the word anymore, you've had too much," he says to me, bringing Ben his drink.

"I can pronounce it! Te–qwee–la," I say, and my hand comes up to mouth. "There is something wrong with my tongue."

Mike smiles and puts a towel over his shoulder. "I'm going to get you some coffee." He walks away.

I look over to Ben, who silently sips his beer.

"You didn't need to come, you know," I say, and try and sit straighter on my stool. "I was going to walk home."

"You wouldn't have made it past the grocers," he says.

"I would have," I say indignantly. "Despite what Mike thinks, I haven't had too much to drink."

He doesn't say anything, which needles me further.

"All the guests have checked out of the Inn," I say and try not to let my voice break.

"I know, your mother called me," he says, still sipping his beer.

"This is probably the end. No one's going to come now."

"You'd be surprised how quickly people move on," he says. "I think you should try and have a little more faith in people."

I snort. "That's the problem. I've had *too* much

faith in people."

He doesn't say anything and I find his silence extremely irritating.

"Let's make a list, okay?" I pick up the napkin in front of me. I search the area for a pen but can't find one anywhere. "I'll just use my finger."

"Maybe it's time we got you home," Ben suggests, and I put my finger to my lips and shush him.

"I'm making a list; I need to concentrate. Okay, number one: my father was a dirty, rotten man-whore that cheated on my mother and left because he picked those women over me."

Ben opens his mouth to say something, but I hold up my hand.

"Number two: I decided to date a man who put his career before me, treated me like shit all the time, and ended up cheating on me with the woman who tortured me in school."

Mike comes and puts coffee in front of me, but I wave him away.

"Number… umm…"

"Three," Ben supplies.

"Right, number three: my Inn, that I dedicated most of my life to restoring, is now temporarily closed for business, and unless a miracle happens, it might permanently stay that way."

I hold up my little napkin with my imaginary writing and look at Ben. "What do you think?" I ask.

"That's one shitty list," he says, nodding.

"It needs a clipboard," I say, looking at the napkin again. "Clipboards make everything better."

"Why don't we take this napkin to your house and find a clipboard for it?" Ben puts money on the counter.

I nod sadly and put my napkin carefully against my chest before getting off the stool. I take one step and the whole room goes round me like a merry-go-round. Except there are no horses. And no candy—just Mr. Phelp's peanuts. This carnival sucks.

I square my shoulders and make my way to the door, finding the cold air refreshing once I am outside.

It feels just like I am at the beach with the breeze blowing on my face, and those hedges are kind of like sand dunes in the dark. I love the beach; I could spend hours there just sitting and relaxing or taking a nice nap.

A nap sounds good right now. I might just lie down a bit on the sand dunes and let the ocean sweep over me.

"Kate, you're lying on a shrub," Ben says as he exits the bar behind me.

"Shhh, I'm listening for seagulls," I say and put

my finger to my mouth to indicate the importance of
it being quiet.

I feel so light, like I am floating over the ground.

Except, I actually am floating over the ground.

I open one eye to see Ben's face. He has me
braced against his chest, his one arm under my legs to
carry me home.

"I can walk," I say.

"No you can't," he argues.

"You're right," I say, smiling, and leaning my
head against his chest. "This is better anyways."

Ben carries me the two blocks to my house and
Maggie greets us at the door.

"Sit Maggie," I say in a sing song voice, and I
open one eye to see her sitting by the door, her head
tilted to the side studying me. "Oh, good doggy!
Ben, isn't Maggie such a good doggy?"

"The best," he says and carries me through the
hallway, pausing by the living room door. "Where's
your bedroom?"

"Maggie, show Ben where our room is," I say
and watch as she gets up and runs down the hallway
to my bedroom. "Good doggy!" I say gleefully and
look up at Ben. "She's a purebred."

We follow Maggie into my bedroom and he sets
me down, putting my head on my yellow, patchwork
pillows.

I watch him look around the room, taking it all in and I beam. "I designed the whole thing myself."

His eyes travel from my rose bud patterned curtains, to my daisy painted dresser I have had since I was born, and finally settles on my bright yellow rocking chair. "My mom used to rock me to sleep in that," I say, looking at it lovingly.

"You picked out all this stuff?" he asks.

"Most of it is from my bedroom when I was a little girl. My mom wanted to throw it out a few years ago when she turned my old room into her zen place, but how could I let her throw this stuff out? It's gorgeous!"

Ben goes over to the rocker and runs his hand over the innate carving on the arm rests before looking at me. "So, this is the girl who used to slide down the banister."

I frown as I look at him and shrug before grabbing my daisy pillow and hugging it to my chest. "I like flowers."

"I figured," he says, coming over to stand beside my bed. He bends down and moves my legs over to make room to sit before he lowers himself onto the edge.

"Greg was sleeping with Samantha," I say.

"I know." he says.

"What? How did you know?" I ask, searching his

face.

"I knew you took something from her apartment, and then when I went to get your inhaler the other day I saw the card on top of your desk," he says.

"That could have been my card," I argue.

He shakes his head. "The corners were all crinkled and there was a bend in the middle like it had been folded in half. If it was yours it would have looked perfect."

I open my mouth to protest, but then close it. He's right. I was even considering ironing it because the crinkles were driving me nuts as I was staring at it all day. "Are you going to arrest him?"

"I don't know. Just because they were sleeping together doesn't prove he murdered her. We need more evidence than that in order to get a warrant."

"She could have been pregnant," I say, looking at him below my lowered eyelids. "I found a test at her place, too."

"She wasn't," he says, shaking his head. "It's one of the first things we look for in an autopsy."

"I just don't understand men," I say, and fresh tears come to my eyes. "There's this box of pictures of the two of them in his apartment, and they looked so... happy together. We never looked like that."

Ben puts his hand on mine for support.

"And I should have known. We haven't had sex in months because he says every time he touches me I get all twitchy. I'm not twitchy, am I?" I ask, looking at Ben as though he holds all the answers.

"No, you're not twitchy," he says.

"He was probably just too busy having sex with Samantha. How was I ever going to compete with that?" I furrow my brow in desperation for answers. "I mean, why did he waste all that time on me when he knew he could do better anyways?"

"He's an idiot," Ben says, looking at his hands.

"I'm an idiot," I say. "My father left me for a bunch of beautiful women, so it's only right my boyfriend did, too."

Ben moves his hands to his sides and looks up at the flowers on my bedroom wall.

"You are the most beautiful thing I've ever seen," he says.

It takes a moment for his voice to register in my slow working brain.

I look at him, not looking at me.

I don't know what to say to that.

His sandy hair is curling at his collar, probably because he hasn't had a haircut in months. His jacket is undone, and the t-shirt's color is bringing out the caramel in his brown eyes.

I slowly sit up and reach out my hand to touch

his hand. The tips of my fingers feel cold as they touch his warm skin.

He takes me in out of the corner of his eye, barely moving his head before my hand reaches up to his face to trail my fingers along his jawline. Leaning forward I stop when my lips are just a few inches from his face, my eyes never leaving his– waiting for him to resist. When my lips finally meet his, I feel a tingling in my stomach that makes my fingertips curl. His lips are soft and full, his skin smells of fresh soap. He frowns as my lips seek encouragement from his, and as I run my hand through his messy, unkempt hair. Suddenly, I feel something inside of him give and his reserved response is gone.

His mouth explores and encourages mine, and even though I've never been a great kisser, Ben seems to be enjoying it. He parts my lips with his tongue and my toes curl as I pull my feet underneath me to make my body closer to his.

I'm not sure if it's the alcohol or Ben's unpredictable thoroughness, but whatever it is, my clipboard loving, order driven, mind throws caution to the wind and grabs at any part of him that I can get my hands on.

I've never been kissed like this before in my life. With Greg it was always so perfect, so planned and precise. He also knew exactly what to do to get a pleasurable result.

But Ben's not like that at all. He's all over the place, his one hand grabbing my cheek, his other on my hip. I don't know what he is going to do next, which is terrifying. But it's also extremely sexy.

I reach for the front of his shirt the same time he reaches for mine, and our hands end up getting tangled trying to get around each other. I let him go first, his fingers working on the buttons of my blouse. My hands grab onto his shoulder and pull him towards me. He finally finishes with my shirt and I reach down to pull the tails of his shirt out of his pants, my mouth never leaving his.

"Wait–" he says, putting his hand over top of mine.

"What, was I twitching?" I ask, my forehead wrinkling.

"No," he says, shaking his head. "You're perfect."

"I read a lot of books for sex advice," I say, my lips trying to reach his again.

"Kate, you're drunk," he says, rubbing his thumb on my cheek.

"It will be better," I say, waving away his concerns. Greg always said I was better when I'd been drinking.

"We can't do this. You would just hate yourself

tomorrow," he says, slowly sitting back up.

I push myself up onto my elbows. "I won't, pinky swear," I say, crossing my heart with my finger.

He looks at me with his skeptical look. "Okay, well I would hate myself tomorrow."

My eyes widen and I quickly close my blouse. "Well I am sorry I would be so disturbing to you tomorrow."

"Not because of *that*," he says, shaking his head. "Kate, I'm not going to take advantage of you."

"Why? I want you to!" I argue.

He stays quiet and I take a deep breath.

Okay, I know I have never been that good at these sorts of things, but I thought I was doing pretty well.

And if he thought tomorrow morning would be awful, it would have been nothing compared to what I'm feeling right now.

"I– umm– I'm kind of tired," I say and try to tamper down the hurt flickering in my eyes.

He studies me for a minute before nodding his head.

"Get some sleep, Kate," he says, leaning over me to get to the lamp on my bedside table. The next thing I know the room is completely black.

And I do sleep.

Thirteen

I awake to a distant ringing in my ears. I slowly open my eyes and look around to find Ben, but the spot beside me is empty. My heart sinks, but then I tell myself it's for the best. I have so many things to deal with this morning that a "what does this mean?" conversation probably is best to leave for another time.

I slowly raise my body from the pillows to test the severity of the pounding in my head, and at once recognize that last night's "teqweela" was a terrible mistake.

I hear loud noises coming from the kitchen, and I force myself to sit upright.

Looking around, I spy my dressing gown on the yellow rocking chair. After brushing my hair I look in the mirror and wince. Maggie has her head on her paws and when she sees me looking, she puts one paw over her eye.

I get it– definitely not a good hair day.

Slowly making my way towards the kitchen, I brace myself for the awkward moment I am about to walk into. I mean, what do you say to a guy when he has told you he can't have sex with you because you're too drunk? I should probably say thank you, except... I'm not so sure that I was that drunk last night. I remember most of it, so how drunk could I have possibly been? But at the same time, it's nicer to my self-esteem to be rejected because of my blood alcohol level than any other reason. You know– the sexually awkward, twitching reason.

But when I finally get through the kitchen doorway, it isn't Ben who is making all the noise.

"Mom?" I ask as I walk into the kitchen. "What's all the commotion?"

"I'm making you breakfast. I can't find the salt." Mom leans inside the bottom cupboard and frantically tries to move around the pots and pans, and they all come crashing out and onto the floor.

"Right, and you're looking in the pots and pans cupboard because...?" I question.

"Because," Mom's mumbled voice comes from inside, "I've looked through all the other cupboards and can't find it anywhere."

Mom emerges from the cupboard, bright red in the face, with her auburn hair tossed every which way. She looks so fresh and natural, and definitely not close to sixty-five. I hope I get a grey streak like her one day.

How could any man not be grateful to have my mother's love?

Maybe the same way I've taken it for granted all this time.

"I just don't understand what happened to it, I could have sworn I saw it on your counter a minute ago." She scans the kitchen counter again.

Frankly, I don't know how she can find anything in here. She seems to have turned the whole kitchen upside down and now everything is just in heaps everywhere. I can see some jelly from a jar slowly inching its way out and getting closer to my new clipboard, and I quickly rescue it before the jelly makes even more of a mess.

"Did you check the kitchen table?" I say in a helpful tone, and look over my shoulder at the salt and pepper shakers sitting neatly in the middle of the small round table.

"There it is!" she says as though she has discovered the greatest mystery. She picks them up and shakes her head. "I've looked everywhere for you."

I scan the room and mentally make a plan to get everything back in its place as quickly as possible, but my thoughts are interrupted by the shrill ring of the phone on the kitchen wall.

"Who keeps calling?" I ask, putting my hand to my temple.

"Greg the Great," Mom says, walking back to the stove and sprinkling salt on the cooking eggs.

At first I take a step back. I'm really not in the right mindset to have it out with Greg right now. For one, I haven't made a list of all the things I am going to say to him.

My mother is singing by the stove, adding a bunch of different herbs to the eggs, and though they look disgusting I'm sure they will taste excellent. Mom's always been a great cook.

She's actually always been good at anything she sets her mind to. She usually does it in a very unconventional way, but she puts her heart and soul into everything she does, and I never appreciate that.

She's spent her life trying to make my dreams come true, sheltering me from the truth about my father, all at her own cost.

If she can deal with all that, I'm sure I can handle a phone call from Greg the Great.

I square my shoulders and charge over to the phone, but my throbbing head reminds me that perhaps charging isn't the best idea today.

"Hello?" I say into the phone.

"Kate? What the fuck is going on? Did you take the last page out of my Tom Clancy novel?" his angry voice yells into the phone.

"Oh, did you need that?" I ask innocently.

"This is exactly why I didn't want to give you a key. I know you're mad that I had to skip out on dinner the other night–"

"Oh, I'm not mad about that," I say, my fingers playing with the phone cord. "I know you'll make it up to me, right?"

Greg stays quiet on the other side of the phone and my resolve to play it cool breaks. I've never been good at playing anything cool.

"I know you were having an affair with Samantha!" I yell into the phone. "And I should warn you the police are pretty sure you were the one who killed her."

"I– what– Samantha is *dead*?" he finally gets out.

"Honestly, the innocent act is so last week." Smiling, I nod at Maggie. I've always wanted to say that, and it came out impeccably, if I do say so myself.

"I didn't kill anyone!" Greg says, and I can hear his voice rise in a slight panic.

"Just like you weren't sleeping with her?" I counter.

Greg pauses again, and then finally sighs into the phone. "Okay, listen Kate. I might have slipped up once or twice–"

I snort into the phone.

"But, I did not kill anyone! I swear to you, this is the first time I've even heard that Samantha is dead," his voice breaks on the last word and I can hear that he is crying on the other side of the phone.

"I'm going to ask you a question and I want you to be honest with me, just this one time," I say. "If you have been sleeping with Samantha this whole time, why did you continue our relationship? We hardly ever see each other– why string me along?"

Greg sighs into the phone. "I do really care about you, Kate. Please believe me. I know I made a mistake–"

"A *mistake*?" I yell.

"Okay, I fucked up. But, it's not like you make it easy to love you," he says.

"*Excuse me?*"

"Nothing in life is ever good enough for you! You kept bitching all the time that you needed a good review for the Inn. So, what did I do? I go out of my way to ask Samantha to come and review it and you go insane trying to please her–"

"*You* asked her to come to the Inn," I say, flabbergasted.

"See, you've never appreciated the things I have done for you. Like all the new things I have tried to get you to try– you just fight me on everything," he argues.

"Oh, I'm sorry," I say, my voice dripping with sarcasm. "Have I not properly thanked you for getting your mistress to come and review the Inn? WHAT DID YOU HAVE TO DO TO GET HER TO AGREE TO THAT?" I yell.

"See, this is exactly what I am talking about," he says.

"You know, if it weren't for the fact that you're a disgusting, cheating liar, I would almost feel sorry for you," I say, gripping the phone cord that is wrapped around my fingers into a tight clenched fist. "But, I don't," I slam down the phone in its holder.

I turn to walk away but my fingers are still tangled in the cord and the phone falls off the wall. I casually pick it up and place it back. It was still a good exit, I reassure myself.

My mother's eyes are wide as she continues to stir the eggs, pretending that she hasn't just heard what happened.

I walk over to where she is standing and put my head on her shoulder.

"Greg the Great and I are not going to be getting married," I say, looking at the disgusting green colour the eggs have turned.

"Oh, really?" she asks in what I'm sure she thinks sounds like regret. "That's too bad."

"Mmm," I say, nodding and taking a piece of egg out of the pan to try. It's actually pretty good.

"Well, there are better fish than him in the sea and at least we won't have to put up with his mother anymore," she says, her one arm wrapped around my back in an embrace. "Ben is quite nice."

"Mother," I sigh, and move my head slightly so my eyes can reach hers.

"What? I'm not saying you have to ask him out this second," she says.

"Greg and I just broke up," I remind her. "And besides, relationships that start out in heated moments like this never work out."

My mother looks back to the eggs and shrugs. "I think when something's good, it's just good. It shouldn't matter how or when it happened."

I study the eggs too. "Was it ever good between you and dad?" I ask.

"Sometimes," she nods. "But not as good as it should have been. I can't really fault your father for doing what he did. We were both unhappy for a long time, and he just wanted to find what we should have had together with someone else before it was too late."

"That doesn't make it right," I point out. "If you're unhappy, then do something about it, but finish what you have started first. A cheater is a cheater, there is no excuse for it," I say adamantly.

"You might be right," she concedes. "But it takes too much energy to stay mad at someone. You hurt yourself more than you hurt them."

A thought suddenly occurs to me and I lift my head and look at my mother. "Was Vivienne one of the women Dad had an affair with?"

My mother's face freezes for a moment before she eventually relaxes and nods her head. "She's the only one I haven't been able to quite forgive, though God only knows why," she shrugs. "I think I could let it go if it weren't for those tacky nails of hers…"

My mom turns back to the stove and turns the gas off.

She's a walking contradiction, and I find myself looking at her and loving her for it.

To stay mad at someone for twenty-something years, not because they slept with your husband, but because of the colour they paint their nails…

My eyes widen, and I grab the counter for support.

That's it.

"Kate, what's wrong?" my mom asks.

"Nothing. I think– I mean, I'm not sure, but I think–" I look around wildly for my purse and remember Ben put it in my bedroom last night. I race over into my room and sift through my purse for my phone.

I click on the photo's icon and find the picture of Samantha's closet.

I stare at it and can't believe my eyes. The answer has been here this whole time.

"Kate, what's wrong?" my mother repeats as she comes into my room, looking at me in concern. Maggie is sitting beside her, looking at me as if to say, "You finally figured it out? I had it a week ago."

"I have to go," I say, grabbing my coat and my purse and running past my mother and Maggie to the front door.

As I turn the doorknob, I open the door and look over at my bewildered mother standing in the front hall– she is desperately trying to catch up with what is going on.

"Call Ben and tell him to meet me at the Inn in half an hour," I say before closing the door and running to my car.

Fourteen

I should have seen it. I mean, I know I have been distracted lately, but usually I am so good at this sort of stuff. I pride myself on being able to spot something out of place. I blame it on not making a list. I would have had it if it was written down.

Samantha's closet had every color of nail polish under the sun, but no red. And there definitely wasn't any red polish in her bathroom at the Inn.

It's a long shot, a *really* big long shot. That's why I have to try and get the confession myself. If I went to the police with this they would *never* be able to prove it. But, I only know one person that is connected to all of this, *and* religiously wears red nail polish. Vivienne.

My mind flashes to Samantha lying on the bed with her bright red nails and I shake my head to get rid of the image. I need to be completely focused if I have any chance of this working.

It's all starting to make so much sense to me. Samantha's apartment décor, the financial backing for the reviews: *that's* how Vivienne became a success overnight. Except, Samantha wrote a bad review for

Viv, and was about to publish it. It would have ruined her.

I call Vivienne and tell her she needs to meet me at the Inn right away. I say I want to talk to her about re-decorating the room that Samantha was killed in. She tries to put me off, saying she is busy at the moment, but I threaten her by saying I will have to get a new designer.

I pull into the Inn and see that her car is already in the parking lot. Ben's isn't anywhere in sight, which makes me slightly nervous. But it's better this way; she won't confess to anything if Ben is around. She probably won't say anything to me either, I realize, but I have a plan.

No list, but a good plan.

Let's see what 'fly by the seat of your pants' Kate can accomplish.

I walk through the Inn and force a warm, welcoming smile onto my face when I see Vivienne standing by the guest book.

"Finally decided to sign in?" I ask, walking up to her and placing a kiss on her cheek.

She shakes her head and smiles in return. "Just seeing what fabulous people have visited our town recently."

"Well, they might be the last for a while," I say and walk to the staircase. "Come on, I'll show you the room."

We walk silently up the staircase and turn right down the hallway. I unlock the door to the room Samantha was staying in and let Vivienne go in first.

"It seems not too long ago that we did this room," she says, putting her purse and coat down on the couch. "But I can understand why you want to redecorate it."

"Mmm," I say, nodding my head. "I was thinking of doing floral drapes."

"No, I don't think that will be right with the lighting in here," she says, getting out her notepad. "You'll want something with stripes, or dark circles on white, like I originally suggested."

My body shakes, and I run my hands up and down my arms. I try to explain it away, "I still get the chills in this room. I mean, someone was *murdered* in here. That's why if we have any chance of reopening we have to redo the whole thing. I can't have the stigma attached to the Inn."

"You're right," she says, nodding.

"I still can't believe it though, can you?" I ask, tilting my head to the side to feign innocence.

"It is rather disturbing," she nods.

"I mean, you hear about these things, but to actually know the person…" I shake my head. "Poor Samantha."

Vivienne shakes her head, "I'm actually surprised no one did it sooner."

"Vivienne, how can you say that?" I ask.

"Honestly Kate, Samantha was a terrible person. I'm sorry, but I just can't muster up any sympathy for her," she shrugs.

"But to die like that..." I say, shaking my head.

She doesn't say anything else and I decide to move on.

"And what do you think about the furniture in here?" I ask, leading her into the bedroom.

I can see her hesitation before she enters the room and I turn to look at the dresser.

"Well, these antiques are beautiful, but I think a more modern, sleek piece would be more beneficial to the wear and tear of the guests."

"And the bed?" I ask.

"Well, naturally you will want to get rid of it since that's where the body was found," she says, and looks around the room. "I think if you got something without a footboard it would open the space up more."

I nod and look around again. "You're probably right."

I step towards the bathroom door, but stop and turn around. "You know, it's funny, I don't remember saying the body was found on the bed."

Vivienne pauses, her eyes losing all warmth before she gently laughs. "Well, I just assumed it was."

I nod my head and smile, "Good guess."

She looks around the room and then closes her notebook. "You know, maybe we should do this another time. Perhaps when you sort out what you are going to do with the Inn," she suggests.

"You're right," I say, walking towards her. I stop when I get to the dresser and run my hand over the top again. "I've always loved antiques. I know they weren't your first choice when we designed the rooms, but I'm glad I went with them."

"They add a certain charm," she concedes.

"I know you like sleeker furniture. It must be the New Yorker in you," I say with a smile.

"Hmm, you know I really do have to run," she says.

"I was so worried that Samantha was going to hate all the furniture I picked in her review. I guess it was a good thing she never did end up writing it," I say.

Vivienne just nods her head.

"I mean, we all know what can happen to a business if a renowned critic doesn't like our work," I say, watching her face.

"I think you put too much stock in what one

woman says," Vivienne says, waving the argument away.

"But you did too, didn't you?" I ask. I see her forehead wrinkle ever so slightly before she shakes her head.

"I don't know what you're talking about."

"I called Mr. Sanders, Samantha's boss, on the way over to offer my condolences about Samantha's death," I lie. "He told me he fired Samantha a week before she came here to write her review. He said he fired her when she wrote a negative review and refused to destroy it. He told me the review was about you."

"That's a lie," Vivienne spits out. "I don't need a review from Samantha Manning; I'm already successful."

"Maybe he was mistaken," I shrug. "Even so, I think I should tell the police, and they can call Mr. Sanders to confirm who the person was. I mean, that review probably cost Samantha her life, so it's only plausible that they will want to talk to the person."

"Wait!" Vivienne says as I take a step forward. "You don't understand."

I see the desperate look on Vivienne's face, partially from fear, but also from something else that I can't quite pin down. Though my gut, the one Ben has been telling me to follow, is very wary of it.

"Then help me," I say.

"I designed that woman's apartment free of charge. Greg got it all set up for me. She was supposed to write an excellent review, and I was going to give the agency her salary for the year."

"But she didn't write an excellent review," I state.

"She was horrendous. And everything she said was a lie!"

"So, she wrote a bad review and you *killed* her?" I ask. I mean, I know I was worried about a bad review as well, but never in a million years would I ever contemplate killing someone because of it.

"You don't get it. I gave her the money, I did everything she asked, but she still wrote a bad review. One that would ruin me! I went to her boss and told him I would not be giving him any money unless it wasn't published, and he assured me it would be taken care of."

"A week later, I come home to get ready for dinner, and there she is sitting on my bed. Painting her nails— with *my* nail polish! She wanted to show me the review she planned on submitting to the New Yorker the next day. Said that she had come to town because she wanted to see my face, so we would both know what it feels like to lose everything." Vivienne takes a step towards me holding out her hand. "She had already decided to ruin you while she was here and tell everyone about her affair with Greg; she said it was an added bonus."

"Did you kill her because of *me*?" I ask, raising my hand to my chest.

Vivienne must see the guilt-ridden look on my face because she bursts out laughing. "Heavens no! I killed her for *me*. I thought maybe she was bluffing, that maybe I could get Greg to speak to her, but then she just kept taunting me at the dinner," she says. "I stole your master key and came up here to talk to her, to offer her more money. When I got to the room though, she wouldn't listen to anything I was saying. She kept telling me it was too late, telling me to get out. I just wanted to make her be quiet so she would listen to me. She just wouldn't shut up."

"Listen Vivienne, you've done a terrible thing, but if you tell the police, I'm sure they'll—"

"Oh Kate," she says walking over to me. "I don't plan on ever telling the police."

I see the hard set look in her eyes and start to take a step back.

"And I can't let you tell them either."

I see the blur of an object before I feel an immense amount of pain on the side of my head.

And then I see nothing at all.

Fifteen

Am I dead? I don't feel dead. But at the same time, I've never been dead before, so I'm not entirely sure what it should feel like.

I open my eye a crack and see a bright light.

Oh God, is that *the bright light?*

I open my eyes a little further and I can see the lamp I picked out at an antique sale last year is turned on.

Oh, good.

Vivienne is sitting on the arm chair in the corner, staring at me. I look around and realize I'm lying on the same bed Samantha died on, and as I try and raise my hand to my forehead I feel the tight pull of the rope around my wrists and groan at the immense pain in my head.

"I'm glad you woke up. I couldn't wait much longer, but I did want you to hear my plan. I know how much you love it when people are organized."

"How–" I cough to clear my throat. "How long have I been out?"

"Oh, just a few minutes. But long enough for me to figure things out."

"What things?" I say, trying to raise my head off the pillow. Vivienne walks over and pushes it back down with her hand.

"I'm afraid I'm going to have to get rid of you, Kate. I can't trust you won't say anything," she looks regretful and then shrugs like it is out of her hands.

"You're going to *kill me?*" I say, shaking my head. "You won't get away with it."

I test the ropes on my hands but they are pretty tight.

"No one will have any reason to believe you have been murdered," she says and picks a piece of rope off the bedside table.

My left hand gives a little as I subtly try and pull on the binding, hoping that Vivienne doesn't see that I am testing the knots she has tied.

"What are you going to do?" I take my eyes off the rope in her hand, focusing on her again.

"I'm not going to do anything," she says, her eyes wide with false innocence. "I came to the Inn, to check on you after the news of the murder got out, and found you in this room. You had hung yourself, because your Inn's reputation is ruined. Everyone will be very sad at your funeral."

"I just don't understand, all this time you seemed like you cared about me, and now you're not going to even blink an eye at killing me?" My eyes fill with confusion and fear.

"Kate, you're a very sweet girl. A little neurotic, but very sweet," she says, patting the side of my face. "I was hoping you would be able to tame my son a little. He's always been so smart, but that girl was always his undoing."

I can see the anger in her eyes and I realize I have to let her vent; I have to keep her talking while I try and free my hand.

"Did you know about Greg and Samantha before she told you that night?" I ask.

Vivienne laughs. "I know everything that my son does: he's never been able to hide anything from me."

"And you never told me?" I ask, and I can't help the hurt in my voice.

Alright, I mean, I know it is a little much to expect loyalty from a woman who is currently trying to kill me, but at the same time I feel like everyone was in on this big secret, and I was the butt of the joke.

"If you found out, Greg would have gone back to pursuing Samantha out in the open. He was devastated when she broke up with him right before college. Even when they were together these past few years, I don't think she would have ever allowed Greg to be a real part of her life. Samantha didn't let anyone in. She was too good for us all," Vivienne says, mockingly.

"So you *both* just used me?" I accuse. My hand slips ever so slightly, gaining slightly with every pull.

"Honey, you allowed yourself to be used," she says. "If you can't hold onto your man, then that's your problem."

"Is that how you justified sleeping with my father?" I ask, and I hate the smile that spreads over Vivienne's face.

"I wondered when she was going to get around to finally telling you," she says, coming closer towards me with the rope. "Now, it has been fun going down memory lane, but I have a two o'clock with my masseuse."

I make a move to avoid her hands, but lifting my head only allows Vivienne to wrap the rope quickly around my neck. She pulls it tight from beside me and my fingers desperately try and escape their binds, wanting to claw away the constriction around my neck. My right hand is useless because she has tied the rope too tight around it, but my left hand has managed to move the rope. I can feel the rough twine digging into my skin as it settles on the wide part of my hand where my thumb and outer knuckle span. The suffocating feeling around my neck is so tight and I can't get any breath. The panicking feeling causes my body to glisten with sweat, and it's all I need to finally free my left hand from its binding. I swing my hand around and manage to strike a fist against her side, but the next thing I know the rope is being pulled down, and Viviane has put her knee on my chest to stop me from moving.

The rope burns into my neck, and the panic makes my hands frantically shake. My eyes plead with her, but she looks so crazed I'm not sure she is paying attention to anything I am doing.

I start to gurgle as the lack of oxygen begins to make my struggles weak. My hand falls to the side, resting on the bedside table, and it encounters cold metal. With the last sap of adrenaline in my body my hand wraps around the antique metal phone, and I swing it in an arc as quickly as I can. When the force hits Vivienne on the side of the head her eyes look confused before she crumples on top of my body.

I roll to the side, forcing her dead weight off of me before I reach for the rope around my neck and finally feel the air enter my lungs.

I reach in my pocket for my inhaler and take a deep breath as soon as it touches my lips.

The door to the suite bursts open and Ben comes rushing inside, first seeing Vivienne's crumpled form, then seeing me with the rope wrapped loosely around my neck.

"Kate!" Ben rushes over and frantically unties my hand. "I heard all the banging– what the hell is going on?"

"Vivienne killed Samantha," I say and try to point at her without looking at her limp body.

"What?" he asks, looking from me to her again.

"She told me everything. Samantha's bad review was about her," I say, following Ben's gaze. "Is she dead?"

"No, I can see she's breathing," he says and releases my right hand to help me up from the bed. "I need to call this in. Let's get you out of here."

Ben leads me out of the room and into the hallway.

"Stay right here, don't move," he orders, and I nod.

He goes back in the room. I look down at my hands but I can't stop them from shaking. That was close. No, close isn't the right word. That was so close it was almost too close.

Never, in all the scenarios that I envisioned in my head, did I think Vivienne might try and kill me. I thought maybe, if I could finally get her to confess, that she would come with me to turn herself in. More than likely though, I thought she would try and run, and I would have to turn her in myself.

I guess I was just banking on the fact that she

cared about me– that she would never hurt me. Well, I was pretty far off with that assumption. So much for being the daughter she never had.

Ben comes out of the room a few moments later.

"She's still passed out, but I handcuffed her to the bed just in case. You must have hit her pretty hard."

I nod absently and he leads me down the stairs, forcing me to sit down at the reception desk.

I hysterically tell him all the things Vivienne confessed to me. I'm so afraid I will forget that I keep repeating the same things over and over again.

He paces up and down in front of me, stopping several times like he wants to say something but just starts pacing again instead.

Finally, he stops in front of me and puts both his hands on the arms of my chair.

"When did you know?" he asks.

"I knew this morning," I say, and then shake my head. "Well, I didn't *know*, I guessed."

"You guessed," he repeats.

"It was the red nail polish on Samantha's fingers. She didn't have any polish that color in her closet at her apartment, and there wasn't any red nail polish in her room here," I say.

He nods his head.

"I knew you would never be able to arrest Vivianne based on nail polish, so I told her to come here so I would get her to confess everything to me."

"And she did?" he asks.

"Yes," I say, nodding my head. "She used Viv's nail polish the night before Vivienne killed her. When I told Vivienne I knew, she told me she had to get rid of me. I never thought..."

"But you got the confession, right?" he asks, his eyes wide with encouragement. "Before she nearly killed you, you got her to confess everything?"

"I did. I even recorded it on my phone, too."

Through his smile I can see his jaw tightening and I frown.

"Are you *mad* at me?"

"No," he says, shaking his head. "Why would you ever think that?"

"You are mad at me," I accuse. "But I caught the bad guy!"

Well, in this case, girl.

"And nearly got killed doing it!" he yells, and then obviously sees me draw back and so tries to calm himself.

"It was the only thing I could do," I argue.

"You could have come to me," he says, pointing to his chest.

"Would you have *believed me*?" I ask. "Even if

you had, she never would have admitted it to you. I needed to catch her off guard."

"That's the point though, isn't it?" he says, shaking his head. "You didn't trust that I would do it properly. You thought that you were the only one that could get it done, and it nearly cost you your life."

"I do trust you!" I say.

"Just like you trusted me enough to tell me about Greg and Samantha? Like you trusted me enough to tell me about the insurance policy?"

I open my mouth in shock.

"How did you know about that?"

"I'm the police; we are sometimes called *investigators*, and are paid to find out these things," he says.

"I couldn't tell you. You would think my mother and I killed Samantha for the money."

"Really?" he asks and sits back on the reception desk. "So, I guess I nearly lost my job trying to protect you and this Inn– keeping it from the media, dressing in costumes, keeping things from my partner and captain– because it's my life's mission to make sure at least one murderer goes free in my career."

"I didn't say–"

"I don't understand you, Kate. You bend over backwards to protect a man that never put you before himself. He stood by while others taunted you, and you thanked him for it," he says, and I can see the anger and hurt in his eyes. "Yet, here I am. I've been standing here, waiting, and you still don't trust me."

"Ben, it's not that I don't trust you, I do. It's just–"

"What if I couldn't get here in time? You could have *died,*" he says and stands up. "I need some air."

"Ben, wait," I say, reaching my hand out for him.

"The police will be here in a minute," he says, walking to the front door and turning the knob. "They'll want to know what happened, so you better work on your story now."

And then the door closes.

I clamp my teeth and try to force back the tears from my eyes.

He wouldn't even listen to me.

Alright, the irony is not lost on me that when he was willing to listen to me I was lying to him or withholding the truth. But still, if he would just listen *now...*

A few minutes later the cavalry arrives, led by Detective Rice. I assure him I'm alright, and he leads the team upstairs to where Ben handcuffed Vivienne to the bed.

I slump in the chair behind the reception desk and the front door opens, my mother racing in.

"Kate!" she runs over to me and wraps me in her arms. "How could you have done that? You could have died," she says, repeating Ben's earlier argument, tears rolling down her face.

"I'm sorry, Mom. It seemed like the only way," I say, and wring my hands over and over in a guilty fashion. "I'm fine."

To be honest, I didn't expect this reaction from everyone. I thought they would be really pleased I found the killer and solved the case.

She looks me over, her eyes briefly stopping on the harsh red marking around my throat and eventually smiles. "We will be," she says.

The next thing I know, I am being taken to the police station. Hours later, after answering the same questions over and over again, I am told by Detective Rice that I'm free to go home. I haven't seen Ben since he went with the team upstairs at the Inn, and as I exit with my mother I notice he isn't around anywhere.

And to be quite honest, I'm not entirely sure I want to see him right now. I mean, I did solve his case for him and I nearly got killed for it! And what thanks do I get? None. He has the audacity to yell at me after all I did for him today.

I don't think he appreciates that this wasn't a walk in the park for me.

Honestly, you nearly sleep with someone because you're drunk, and he happens to tell you that you're the most beautiful thing he has ever seen... and what... that gives him the right to tell you what to do?

The least he could have done was say thank you.

As I sit in the passenger seat of my mother's car I realize that this is the end. Samantha's murder is solved.

So, why don't I feel happy?

Sixteen

This whole thing is ridiculous. I'm never listening to my mother again. She's been nagging me to come here for the last two weeks, and though it is what I want to do, my fear keeps arguing with her.

I stand in the front section of the police station, my eyes anxiously darting around to all the busy faces. No one looks up from their desk.

Honestly, what if this was a real emergency? They really should have a reception desk with a bell. I wonder if there is a suggestion box around here somewhere.

"Need help with something?" A woman looks up at me from her desk.

"I– umm– I'm looking for Be– er– Detective Gable," I say, and awkwardly move my weight from one foot to the other.

"Ben!" she yells at the top of her lungs.

My face goes red as head after head looks up from their desks.

"Oh, okay. Thanks," I say as she looks back at me and smiles before continuing her work.

I look up and see Ben weaving through the

desks, his eyes never leaving my face. His sandy hair is messy, as always, and his shirt looks like he has slept it in all week. His face is a blank mask.

"Er– Hi," I say and hold out the box in my hands. "This is for you."

He takes the box and lifts the lid. "Donuts?"

"My mom said you would like them," I try to control the blush spreading along my cheeks. "I wanted to get you an agenda."

"You didn't have to get me anything," Ben says, turning around to put the box down on someone's desk.

"I wanted to say thank you," I say. "For everything you did for me."

"It's my job," he says, and I tell my heart not to be disappointed at his words.

"Well, I still appreciate it," I say. I look around the station, and although no one is looking in our direction, I still feel like I am being watched. "Could we… umm… could I talk to you? Somewhere a little more private?"

He raises his eyebrow but doesn't object. He leads me into one of the rooms off the main entry.

The room has a single table in the center with a chair on each side. Neither of us makes a move to sit down, so I take a deep breath and turn to face him.

"Listen, I just didn't want things to end the way

they did between us. I… umm… I didn't want you to think that just because I went behind your back, I don't trust you."

He doesn't say anything so I keep talking.

"I do trust you," I say, just in case he didn't get that bit.

He nods his head. "Okay."

I clench my teeth slightly but then tell myself to relax. I mean, I didn't expect him to make this easy.

"I just wanted you to know that I know you stuck your neck out for me for the past few weeks, and I should have come to you with my suspicions."

He stares at me and I can't tell what he's thinking. He's being annoyingly relaxed. And after I brought him donuts!

"Is that all?" he finally asks.

My temper flares at his flippant tone.

"No! I came here to say thank you, and I'm not even sure why I bothered," I put my hands on my hips.

"Well, you've said thank you already," he points out.

"I also came to ask you if you would like to– I mean, if you're not busy sometime–" I say, but I just can't manage to get the words out. If he wasn't being such a jerk…

He continues to stare at me, watching my

agitated movements.

"I don't even know why I bothered though! I made a very thorough pros and cons list, and the results weren't good," I say, throwing my arms in the air. "It would never work out between the two of us. You're messy, disorganized, your hair is all over the place, you never iron your shirts, and it drives me nuts when you touch my business cards."

I look down after my angry outburst and take a deep breath before looking into his eyes. "But I like you. You drive me crazy, but I like you. And I wanted to know if you were free sometime, maybe you would like to go out with me."

He studies my agitated movements and I try and stop my eye from twitching. Which is completely his fault, if he hadn't got me so worked up…

When he finally opens his mouth, the door opens and Detective Rice pops his head in.

"Sorry to interrupt, but the Captain wants to see you right now Ben. He's pissed off about the Capley case."

"Okay," he says, nodding, and turns back to me.

"It's okay," I say, moving my purse higher onto my shoulder. "I'm sorry, I shouldn't have come."

I give Detective Rice a forced smile as I walk past him, back into the main office area. The lid on the box of donuts is open and there isn't a pastry left inside.

Mom was right again.

I really don't feel like going to the Inn, but I promised Mom I would stop by today after I went to the police station. She said she had exciting news and needed to talk to me, but I know she just wants to check up on me and see if things worked out between Ben and me.

I pull into the parking lot and look at my Inn. It's been over two weeks since the incident and I haven't stepped inside since.

I haven't been avoiding it.

I just needed time to, you know, come to terms with everything. Though I'm not sure I've really come to terms with anything yet, which is why coming here is a really bad idea.

Mom has been looking after everything for me, though there really isn't anything to look after. We haven't had one guest check in for the last two weeks, and as far as I know, no one has booked for the upcoming holidays either.

Yet, I reassure myself.

It's not over until it's over.

And I refuse to believe it's over.

I have come up with some great ideas over the past few weeks while I've been at home, and I think I might be on to something.

So far I've got:

1. Hire Martha Stewart to come and stay at the Inn, give a great endorsement, and be swamped with all the new reservations.

2. Hire Simon Cowell (I would even settle for Demi Lovato at this point) to come and stay at the Inn, give a great endorsement, and be swamped with all the new reservations.

3. Hire Meryl Streep (This is really my number one choice, but I have not been properly assured by my mother that she will act appropriately and not stalk poor Meryl) to come and stay at the Inn, give a great endorsement, and be swamped with all the new reservations.

I feel I have a solid plan. Now all I have to do is get someone to return my phone calls, which honestly I blame on the lack of coordination in the entertainment industry. When I questioned Meryl's assistant if she really had written down my number, she hung up on me.

I gather my bag and walk to the front doorway of the Inn. It looks just as beautiful as it did the day we opened; my mom has even put our holiday wreath up, and strung the twinkle lights on the trees outside.

My heart sinks, but I shake off the feeling.

Whatever it takes, I am going to save our Inn.

I open the front door, hear the familiar jingle of the welcoming bell, and see my mom and Tracy behind the reception desk.

The guest book is sitting on the hall table, the reception desk is gleaming, and my business cards are sitting straight. I breathe in the smell of apples and cinnamon, and feel I am home.

"Honey! You're finally here. We've been waiting for you," Mom says and shoots Tracy a sly smile.

"Well, I'm here," I say. "What's the big news?"

"Well–" my mother starts.

"Your mother has done it!" Tracy squeals with excitement. "The Inn is saved!"

"What?" I look at my mother.

"That was my line," she frowns at Tracy.

"Tell her, then," Tracy says, gesturing her arms towards me.

"Well, I know you have been saying we need a good endorsement to fight the bad publicity," my mother says.

"And she got it!" Tracy blurts out then immediately covers her mouth.

"You did it again!" my mother says to her.

"Sorry," she shrugs guiltily, but looks too pleased with the events.

"You got Meryl Streep?" I say in disbelief, dropping my bag to the ground.

"No," my mother says regretfully. "Though her assistant did promise that I will be Meryl's first call when she gets back from Vale... wonderful woman."

"So, who did you get, then?"

"I got—"

"Oh, you're going to be so excited!" Tracy cries.

"Are you telling the story, or am I?" My mom turns to her with her hands on her hips.

"Okay, okay," Tracy says, "you tell her."

"Someone tell me!" I say, throwing up my arms.

"I got—" my mother turns to Tracy to makes sure she isn't going to interrupt her before she turns back to me, her face animated, "Dr. Chural."

They both look at me with huge smiles on their faces, waiting for my reaction.

"*Who?*"

My mother shakes her head. "Dr. Chural! Honestly Kate..."

"Should I know who that is?" I ask. I'm not very up on the latest celebrity gossip. I haven't been able to bring myself to read magazines since Brad and Jen broke up. I know it's old news, but it still hurts.

"Dr. Chural is only one of the leading plastic surgeons in New York City," Tracy says, clasping her hands together.

"What does that have to do with the Inn?" I ask. Obviously I have missed something, because the way Tracy and my mother are acting you would think they'd got Meryl. And don't get me wrong, I'm desperate at this point, so I will take doctor whoever if he is willing to come.

But, I did have my heart set on Meryl.

"He's going to endorse our Botox treatment program!" My mother says.

"Our *what?*"

"Our Botox treatment program," she says. "I told you about it a few weeks ago."

"And I said I would think about it," I say, looking from her to Tracy.

"Well, you thought about it and you never said no, so I figured that was a yes," she says.

"That's not what it means," I say. Honestly, my mother can be exasperating. "Where would we even do it? We only have one room in the spa."

Tracy and my mother look at each other again but they don't seem as enthusiastic as before.

"What?" I ask.

"Well, we… umm… expanded a little," my mom says.

"You what?"

"We expanded," she says. "We converted the boarded up rooms into four treatment rooms, a sauna and expanded the main entryway in the spa to accommodate the manicure and pedicure stations."

My eyes go wide. "You *did* the renovation, or you *plan* on doing the renovation?"

"We... umm... we did it," my mother says. "Tracy agreed with me."

Tracy opens her mouth to protest, but my mother shoots her a look.

"Where did you get the money from?" I ask, trying to control my temper.

"We got all that money from the insurance company," Mom says, her tone getting a little lighter. "So really, it's like the renovation was free."

Thank god my mother isn't in charge of doing our accounting.

"Mom, it doesn't work like that! I was planning on using that money until we figure out some way of getting new reservations."

"Well, I already told you how we are going to get the reservations," she says as though I'm not following.

"Mom, we live in Summerside. People here won't get Botox, and even if they would they would never admit to it! Mrs. Phelps was nearly ostracized last year when she was caught using pesticides on her lawn!"

It's true. The poor woman nearly had to move.

It probably didn't help that her neighbor's dog ate her flowers and nearly died.

"Yes, I don't suppose people that live here would come in for Botox," my mother admits.

"This is exactly why I have a suggestion box! You haven't thought this through properly and you've already done all the renovations."

Oh God, I need to sit down.

"Katherine Foster, you never have any faith in me!" my mother accuses.

Okay, maybe that statement is slightly true. But she obviously doesn't see that right now might not be the best time to bring up this argument.

"Okay, it's going to be okay," I say, bringing my hand to my forehead. "You didn't use all the money, right?"

My mom and Tracy exchange guilty looks.

"*Right?*" I repeat.

"Of course not," Tracy says, looking at my mom. "There's some money left, right Tara?"

"Yes, definitely." My mom doesn't make eye contact with me.

"How much?"

"Oh... I don't know the *exact* amount... We had to pay extra to have it done so quickly..."

"*How much?*"

"Twenty-five dollars," she admits. "But I just

ordered some new magnetic nail polishes so I actually need five dollars out of petty cash to cover the shipping."

"Oh God," I say, leaning on the wall for support. "We're done."

"Of course we're not," my mother argues.

"Mother, I'm not sure if you are grasping this, but we run an Inn. And the purpose of an Inn is to house paying guests. Do you see any guests?" I wave my hands around.

"Well, of course not. They aren't due until Friday; that's when the renovations will be complete," she says.

Oh god, she's actually gone delusional.

"What are you talking about?"

"The guests," she slows her speech, and I feel we are both equally confused with each other. "They are checking in this weekend. We are fully booked."

I open my mouth to say something, but nothing comes out.

"Dr. Chural endorsed the program that Tracy made for our guests, and some of his clients are coming from New York for the weekend. Dr. Chural says that if they love it, we will be set for life," she says. "Apparently New York woman have extensive social circles, most of whom want to stay young and rejuvenated."

"And we have the perfect setting," Tracy joins my mother's pitch. "They can come to Summerside to relax and get away from it all. Plus, we are far enough away from New York, and we've made our treatment rooms very private, so if a client wants full disclosure, they can have it."

I shake my head. I have nothing to say.

"We will still have guests staying with us that will just be enjoying our spa, or visiting the area," my mother argues. "But this way we can be very busy during the week as well. Most of the women want the work done while their husbands are away on business."

"Dr. Chural himself is coming this weekend," Tracy says, clapping in excitement. "He's going to watch me do the first procedure so he can endorse it in good conscience."

"So," my mother says, wrapping the front of her flowing kimono around her finger. "What do you think?"

"How did you even get this doctor to agree to do this?" I ask.

"Tracy sent him the basket full of soap that was meant for Samantha," Mom says, her arm wrapping around Tracy's shoulder. "Apparently he hasn't been sleeping well, and after his bath he had the best night sleep he's ever had."

"I–" I shake my head, tears glistening in my eyes.

"You're upset," my mother says. "I should have talked to you about it first, but I just wanted to surprise you."

I take one step, then another until I am in front of Tracy and my mother and have wrapped my arms around both of them.

"Thank you," I manage to say.

"We just wanted to make your dreams come true," my mother says, choking up herself. "This Inn is your life."

"Our dreams," I say, hugging them both tighter. "And I love this Inn, but I have much more important things in my life as well."

"Oh God, if your mother hadn't just injected my crow's feet I would definitely be crying right now," Tracy sniffles as we stand behind the reception desk.

"But what about the other investors?" I ask my mother. "Please tell me you ran this past them."

"They were fine with it," she waves her hand.

"Were they really, or did they say they would think about it, too?" I ask. "Maybe I should just call them to make sure."

"You can't," she says, avoiding my eyes. "They're in... umm... Istanbul."

"Istanbul? Who do you know that's from Istanbul?" I argue. "Anyways, they still have phones there."

"Well, they can't take any calls," she says. "They don't participate in anything modern."

"But they were okay with *Botox*?" I ask.

When my mother avoids my eyes I know something is up.

"Mother…"

"Alright," she says, sighing. "There are no other investors."

"What? Where did you get the money for the Inn?"

"I got it from your father's estate when he died. He left me a million dollars to spend however I saw fit," she says.

"*What*? Why didn't you tell me?" I ask.

"Because, you love this Inn. You loved it from the second you saw it when you were a little girl, and even after your father left you were determined to own it," she says. "I knew the truth would someday come out about him, and I didn't want where the money came from to taint your love of this place."

I study my mother's guilty face.

"So we own the Inn? Just me and you? It's all ours?"

"And Tracy, I gave her ten percent for getting the endorsement," she says.

I look at Tracy, who shrugs her shoulders, and

has a huge smile on her face.

"This is it, right? There are no more secrets that you plan on springing on me later?" I ask, but at this point I'm not really sure what to believe.

"That's it, I swear," my mom says. "Except for the fact that I broke the oven in the kitchen making homemade candles yesterday. But that's it."

I nod and put my bag on the reception desk. Turning back I grab both my mother and Tracy's hands.

"So... we own the Summerside Inn," I say, looking around the front entryway. "And it's fully booked through to the New Year with famous, rich New Yorkers?"

"I guess we do," Tracy says, equally in awe.

I stand there nodding.

"Happy dance?" I ask.

"Definitely," my mom replies.

We spend the next five minutes doing a lot of movements that are neither dignified nor coordinated.

It was the best moment of my life.

Seventeen

Who knew a month could go by so quick, and so slow at the same time?

To say my mother was right would be an understatement. The Inn is so busy that I've had to make more and more lists to get everything done. So, of course I'm in Heaven.

The reviews from the first weekend were unbelievable, and we are booked up through Valentine's Day with our spa treatments. And people are telling other people who are telling other people. They love the quaint charm of our Inn and town. Everyone also happens to love my guest book; I've had to make a second edition to accommodate all the new names. The first one is in our hutch in the dining room, displayed proudly.

Surprisingly, not a lot of people ask about Samantha, and those that do don't have a lot of nice things to say. I actually find myself feeling sorry for her during these moments. I mean, it's sad that you live your whole life and when it's over, no one misses you. I make sure to give my mom a hug any chance I can get now. I'm not willing to go out that way.

I haven't heard from Greg, which is not surprising. He has tried to separate himself from the town and the whole situation. Apparently it's bad for his image.

I don't blame him for anything, really. I was too blinded to see what I should have all along. No matter what I was led to believe, I have always been better than the Samantha and Gregs of this world.

And Ben was right: Greg should have stood up for me all those years ago, and the fact that he didn't means we were never meant to be. Thank God!

And then there is Ben. I haven't heard from him. Which is...

Well, it is what it is.

I screwed it up.

But, if I ever get the chance again— if someone like Ben comes along again— well, I will know what to do.

We just never had the right timing; never said the right things.

But I have to move forward. No more trying to change the past. I have a fabulous Inn to run, and everyone is depending on me.

I also still haven't heard from Meryl.

"Kate, Mr. Shaw wants to know if his dog can be in the room while I do his forehead," Tracy says, her eyes wide and pleading as Mr. Shaw stands behind her, clutching his Chihuahua.

"I've explained to him that it is against the Inn's policy to even have animals as guests, let alone in the room during a session," she says, smiling, trying to hide the clenching of her teeth.

"Mr. Shaw..." I say, turning to him.

"I'm just so nervous," he says, stroking the dog a little more forcefully than necessary. "And poor Pinky can pick up when I'm nervous. I don't want him to worry."

"I'll tell you what," I say, waving to Becky as she passes by with her arms loaded with towels. "I'll get Becky to light some of her special incense in the room. It is specifically designed to relax the nerves. And she can take, umm... Pinky, for a walk while you have your session."

He squints his eyes to look at Becky, who smiles over the towels. "Alright, but not too far. And don't walk him around a lot of other big dogs, he gets depressed," he says.

Becky nods as I take the towels from her hands.

"And make sure you stop every twelve minutes for a water break, he only drinks reverse osmosis..." I miss the rest as Becky walks with Mr. Shaw and Tracy back to the spa.

"Where is that girl going?" Luisa asks, coming towards me and taking the towels.

"I've asked her to walk Mr. Shaw's dog," I say.

"I guess I do the baños myself then," she says, shaking her head.

"I'll help you," I offer, seeing that a meltdown might be coming.

"No, no, you don't do it right," she says and disappears around the corner.

Honestly, how can you not clean a bathroom right?

My bathroom seems perfectly clean at home.

I'll have to write that on my list, see what I'm doing wrong.

"Honey, I've told Mrs. Thorn that we can make tonight's trifle diabetic friendly," she says, coming to the front desk and picking up the mail.

"But we can't," I argue.

"Can't we just ask Cook to take out the sugar?" she asks.

"No, it will taste horrible for everyone else," I say.

"Oh well, I'll just tell her its diabetic friendly then," she says shrugging.

"Mother, you can't do that!" I argue. "What if she has an episode because of it?"

"Oh she'll never notice, and I saw her eating a Mars Bar last night. She just tells everyone she's diabetic for attention," she puts down the mail and kisses me on the cheek. "Honestly, the woman is a nightmare."

She walks away and I make a note on my clipboard to investigate the diabetic thing. Just in case.

The front door bell chimes as I am finishing my note.

I look up and smile to greet our new guest, but drop my pen when I see Ben standing in front of the reception desk.

My mouth opens, but no sound comes out.

"Hello," he says, smiling.

His face is just as handsome as I remember, probably even more so. He's tried to comb his hair into a semblance of order, but it doesn't look right. I want to reach my hand up and shake it all out of place the way it should be. His shirt is wrinkled, and he's tried to tuck it into his jeans but one of the front shirt tails has escaped and is hanging loose at the front.

"I–" I still have no idea what to say. What are you supposed to say in situations like this? You know, for someone who lives a well-organized life, I'm shocked with what little I have been prepared for in the past few months. Maybe I need to get out more.

"I brought you something," he says, putting a

gift bag on the desk, pushing my business cards to the side.

I look at him warily before reaching in the bag and pulling out a florescent pink clipboard.

"I thought it might be time for you to spice things up a little," he says, smiling, and waiting for my reaction.

I hold the clipboard in my hands, staring at it. I reach for the clipboard I was just writing on, take off the paper, and put it on my new pink one.

"Thanks," I say, holding the clipboard against my chest.

"So, how are things?" he asks as Becky walks by with Pinky who is wearing a miniature sombrero.

"His eyes are sensitive to the sun," Becky says, shrugging before going out the front door.

"Pretty much the same," I say, smiling. "Except everything has changed as well. We have expanded the spa and reached out to new clientele. Things are great."

"I've heard," he says, smiling and looking around at the bustling Inn. "I'm really happy for you, Kate."

"It was mostly my mom and Tracy" I say. "I'm just here to make sure they don't burn the place down."

"The last thing you need is another investigation," Ben guesses with a smile.

"The last one wasn't so bad," I offer and lower my eyes.

"Well, I have the weekend off and I was wondering if you had a vacancy," he says.

My eyes shoot up to study his face, wondering what this means, but he doesn't give anything away.

"We only have your old room available," I say. "We just finished redecorating it yesterday, so we didn't book it out this weekend yet."

My mom and I have spent the last few weeks going to antique auctions picking up some great finds. Some we got for great prices; others I practically had to sit on top of my mother's hand to stop her from raising the paddle when someone was trying to bid her up. She can get a *little* competitive.

"Sounds good," he says. "Do I need to fill out the form again?"

"We should have your old one on file." I say, writing his name in my reservation book. "How long will you be staying?"

"It depends," he says. He puts down his bag at the side of the reception desk and leisurely makes his way around until he is standing in front of me.

I try not to get my hopes up. Maybe he is just here to be polite. He has always loved the Inn, maybe he just wanted to stay here in its heyday.

"On what?" I ask, my eyes never leaving his face.

"On you."

My heart flutters at his words, but I mustn't get ahead of myself.

"I'm not sure what *I* would have to do with it," I say, shrugging my shoulders. "You made it clear a month ago that I wasn't going to be a factor in your life."

"Did I say that?" he asks, frowning.

"You didn't have to say it. The fact that I haven't seen you in over a month says it all," I argue.

He nods, running his hands through his once again messy hair.

"I had to go away for a little while to work on a case; the one my captain wanted to talk to me about that day you came to see me. But even so, what if I told you I didn't come here the next second, the next day, the next week after you left the station because I wanted to give you time to make sure *you* were sure?" he asks.

"Well, I would say that is stupid," I say, crossing my arms.

"You made some excellent points as to why we shouldn't be together. You weren't sure if it would work between the two of us," he points out.

"Well, what do I know?" I say, my angry eyes meeting his.

"You seem to know everything," he says,

shrugging. "You're a perfectionist, obsessively organized, you color coordinate your pens, and you might be the slowest driver I have ever met."

I open my mouth to argue, but his arms wrap around me and my voice catches. Alright, he might be *slightly* right about some things.

But I am not a slow driver. Slow and cautious aren't the same thing.

"But because of all that, I love you. More than I have every loved anyone in my entire life. And I was wondering if you are free sometime, you might give me the chance to make you love me, too."

"I–" my breath catches as he tucks a lose strand behind my ear. "I think I already might."

"You're sure?" he asks. "You don't want to make another pros and cons list?"

"It was already leaning in your favor," I admit as I wrap my arms around his shoulders. "The clipboard just tipped it over."

His face lowers, his lips soft as he presses them to mine. I can feel the passion within him, so earnest and unheld. He's such a contradiction, and that's my favorite thing about Ben. A warmth envelops me and I respond just as passionately.

He lifts his head from mine, and brings his hands up to my face. He lovingly takes in every one of my features before placing another tender kiss on my mouth.

"Oh, you kids are just adorable," my mom says, and she ruffles Ben's hair as she passes the reception desk.

"Hi Tara," Ben says, still smiling at me.

"I see you managed to work things out," she says and winks at me before she rounds the corner to disappear into the next room.

"So, are you going to show me to my room?" Ben asks, running his hands up and down my arms, sending thrilling chills all over my body.

"Mmm," I say, as he pulls back and drops his hands to my waist. "But first things first. You have to sign the guest book."

His mouth lifts at the corner before he nods. "Nearly forgot."

While he makes his way around the reception desk, I lean over and straighten my business cards so they are parallel with the edge of the desk again.

"Where do I sign?" he asks, looking at the book pages, before starting to scribble his name.

I come to stand behind him and peek over his shoulder. "You've done it in the wrong spot!" I say, trying to step in front of him. "You're not visiting a friend, you're checking in."

"Okay," he shrugs and starts to cross out his name in the wrong column.

"No!" I say, putting my hand on top of his. "You'll make the book messy."

"So, we'll pretend I'm visiting, then?" he asks with an indulgent smile.

"Then the records won't be right," I say, weighing up my options. "You'll just have to sign in on both columns."

"Are you going to scrunch your nose like that every time I do something you find annoying?" he asks.

I look from him, to the book, back to him.

"Yes."

"Good," he says, smiling before capturing my lips again.

OTHER BOOKS BY EMILY HARPER

Natalie Flemming is searching for the man of her dreams. She is craves adventure, spontaneity, passion– or will just settle for a decent date.

"I highly recommend 'White Lies' – it's a quick and very entertaining read!"- Untitled Views

Available through Amazon and all major retailers.

ABOUT THE AUTHOR

Emily Harper, author of White Lies and Checking Inn, has a passion for writing humorous romance stories where the heroine is not your typical damsel in distress. Throughout her novels you will find love, laughter, and the unexpected!

Originally from England, she currently lives in Canada with her wonderful husband, beautiful daughter, mischievous son, and a very naughty dog.

Visit her website: http://emilyharper.wordpress.com